Third Year at Malory Towers

This is the third book
in the Malory Towers series

✔ KU-523-704

This Armada book belongs to:

WILMSHURST
BIRCHDALE
THE GREEN
PITTON
SALISBURY SP5 1DZ

Enid Blyton

Third Year at Malory Towers

ARMADA

First published in the UK in 1948
by Methuen & Co. Ltd
Republished by Dragon Books in 1967
First published in Armada in 1988
This impression 1993

Armada is an imprint of
HarperCollins Children's Books,
part of HarperCollins Publishers Ltd,
77–85 Fulham Palace Road,
Hammersmith, London W6 8JB

Printed and bound in Great Britain by
HarperCollins Manufacturing, Glasgow

A New Girl for Malory Towers

Darrell was busy helping her mother to pack her clothes to take back to boarding school. Her little sister Felicity was watching, wishing that she too was going with Darrell.

"Cheer up, Felicity!" said Darrell. "You'll be coming back with me in September. Won't she, Mother?"

"I hope so," said her mother. "Miss Grayling said she thought she would have room for her then. Oh, Darrell, surely you don't want all those books! They make your trunk so heavy."

"Mother, I do!" said Darrell. "And do let me take back my roller skates. We're allowed to skate round the courtyard now. It's such fun."

"All right," said Mrs Rivers. "But it means unpacking half the trunk, because they must go at the bottom. Oh dear – did we mark your new bedroom slippers?"

"No!" groaned Darrell. "Felicity, be a darling and mark them for me. Matron absolutely goes off the deep end if she finds anything not marked."

Felicity darted off to get a pen. She was eleven and Darrell was fourteen. How she longed to go to Malory Towers too! According to Darrell it was the finest school in the kingdom!

"I wish we hadn't got to call for that new girl," said Darrell, bent over her trunk. "What's her name now, Mother? I keep forgetting it."

5

"Zerelda," said her mother. "Zerelda Brass."

"Golly!" said Darrell. "Zerelda! Whatever will she be like?"

"Oh, all right, I expect," said Mrs Rivers. "She's American, you know. But her English grandmother has asked her over here for a year, and she's to go to Malory Towers. It's a marvel they were able to take her at short notice like that."

"What's she like?" asked Darrell. "Have you seen her?"

"No. Only a photograph," said Mrs Rivers. "She looked about twenty there! But she's only fifteen, I think."

"Fifteen! Then she won't be in my form," said Darrell. "She'll be in one higher up. Mother, isn't it a shame Sally's in quarantine for mumps? She'll be late coming back."

Sally Hope was Darrell's best friend at school. Usually they arrived together at Malory Towers, for either Darrell's father or Sally's drove them down together in their cars. But this time Sally would be late because of the mumps quarantine.

"You'll have to write and tell her everything," said Mrs Rivers. "Oh, thank you, Felicity – you've marked the slippers beautifully. Have you put in your dressing gown, Darrell? Oh yes, there it is. Well, now we're really getting on. Where's the list? I'll just run down it and see if we have left anything out."

"If Sally hadn't been in quarantine we wouldn't have had to call for Zerelda," said Darrell. "There wouldn't have been room. Mother, I have a feeling she will be awful. Whatever shall we talk about to her all the way down to Cornwall?"

"Good gracious – can't you talk about Malory

Towers?" said her mother. "You seem to be able to talk about it for hours on end at home."

At last the packing was all done. Then there was the usual hunt for the key of the trunk, which always disappeared regularly each holiday.

"Have you signed my health certificate, Mother?" asked Darrell. "Where is it? In my nightcase? Right. I wonder if Irene will have got hers safely this term?"

Felicity giggled. She loved hearing about the harum-scarum Irene who always started off safely with her health certificate, and could never find it when she arrived.

Darrell's father was driving with her mother and Darrell down to Malory Towers the next day. They had to start early, so all the packing was done the day before. All that Darrell had to do the next day was to go round the house and garden with Felicity and say goodbye to everything, even the hens!

"I shan't have to say goodbye to *you* in September, Felicity," said Darrell. "Well, goodbye, now, and just see you get on well in games this term, so that I can be proud of you when you come to Malory Towers!"

They were off at last, purring away down the road to the West Country. It was a lovely day in January, cold and sunny. Darrell pulled the rug round her. She was sitting alone at the back of the car. Her mother was in front. Soon they would come to Zerelda's house and then Darrell would have her at the back with her.

Zerelda lived in a big house about fifty miles along the way. Her grandmother had been a great friend of Mrs Rivers' mother, and it was really Darrell's granny that had asked Mrs Rivers if she could fetch Zerelda and take her down to the school with Darrell.

"I think it would be so nice if she and Darrell could

7

have a good long talk about the school," said Darrell's granny. "Zerelda is sure to feel a bit strange, going to a school in a different country."

But Darrell didn't feel very pleased about it. She was disappointed that they couldn't fetch Sally, her friend, and somehow she didn't like the sound of Zerelda. Was it the unusual name? Or was it that she felt her mother didn't altogether like the sound of Zerelda either? Anyway, they would soon see!

"Here's Notting," said Mr Rivers, seeing the name on a signpost. "This is where we call for the American, isn't it?"

"Yes," said Mrs Rivers, looking at the card in her hand. "Turn to the right by the church. Go up the hill. Turn to the right again at the top and you will see a big white house. That's where Zerelda is living."

They soon drew up at a big white house, almost a mansion. A butler opened the door. Then a smart, little old lady came running out, the friend of Darrell's granny.

"This *is* kind of you!" she said. "Zerelda! Are you ready? Here they are."

No Zerelda appeared. Mrs Rivers said they wouldn't come in and have coffee, as they wanted to be at the school before dark.

"If Zerelda is ready, we'll set off straight away," said Mr Rivers. He felt a little annoyed. Where was this Zerelda? She ought to have been ready and waiting! He went to the back of the car and got ready a strap for the luggage.

"Zerelda! Come at once!" called her grandmother. She turned to the butler. "Do you know where Miss Zerelda is? Oh dear, where can she be?"

It was some minutes before Zerelda appeared. And

when she did arrive Darrell couldn't think that it *was* Zerelda! She suddenly saw a tall, willowy person come down the stairs, with glinting hair the colour of brass, arranged in a big roll on the top of her head, with curls cascading over her shoulders.

Darrell stared. Who was this? She looked like somebody out of the films. And, good gracious, she had lipstick on surely?

It couldn't be Zerelda. This girl looked about twenty. She came forward with a lazy smile.

"Oh! Zerelda! Where were you?" said her grandmother. "You've kept us waiting."

"Sorry," drawled Zerelda. Her grandmother introduced her to the Rivers family. Mr Rivers looked impatient. He hated to be kept waiting – and he didn't like the look of Zerelda much!

Neither did Darrell. In fact, she felt quite alarmed. Zerelda must be seventeen or eighteen at least! Whatever would they talk about in the car?

"You'd better put on your school hat," said her grandmother, handing it to Zerelda.

"What! Wear that terrible thing!" said Zerelda. "Gee, Gran'ma, I never shall!"

Darrell didn't dare to say that she would certainly have to. She was quite tongue-tied. Zerelda seemed really grown-up to her. It wasn't only her looks, and the way she did her hair – it was her self-confident manner, and her grown-up way of talking.

She slid gracefully into the seat by Darrell. "Now, Zerelda, you remember you're going to an English school, to learn a few English ways," said her grandmother, at the window of the car. "Oh dear, wipe that lipstick off your mouth. I've told you again and again it won't do here. You seem to think you're eighteen,

9

but you're only a schoolgirl. Now mind you . . ."

Mr Rivers, feeling that talk between Zerelda and her grandmother would probably go on for some time, put in his clutch and revved up the car. "Goodbye!" said Mrs Rivers, feeling that they might stay for ever if she didn't firmly say goodbye.

The car moved off. Zerelda's grandmother was left still talking at top speed in the drive. Mr Rivers heaved a sigh of relief, and looked at his wife out of the corner of his eye. She looked back. Darrell caught the look and felt a little comforted. Daddy and Mother thought the same about Zerelda as she did!

"Have you got enough rug?" Darrell asked politely.

"Yes, thanks," said Zerelda. There was a silence. Darrell racked her brains to think what to say.

"Would you like me to tell you something about Malory Towers?" she asked Zerelda at last.

"Go ahead, honey," said Zerelda, rather sleepily. "Spill the beans. What's our class teacher like?"

"Well – you won't be in my class, because you're fifteen, aren't you?" said Darrell.

"Nearly sixteen," said Zerelda, patting the big roll on the top of her head. "No, I guess I won't be in your class. You're not very big are you?"

"I'm as big as anyone else in my form," said Darrell, and she thought to herself that if she wore her hair in the same ridiculous way as Zerelda did, she too would look tall.

She began to talk about Malory Towers. It was her favourite subject, so her voice went on and on, telling about the great school with its four big towers, one at each end – the courtyard in the middle – the enormous pool in the rocks, filled by the sea each tide, where the girls bathed in the summertime.

10

"And in each tower are the dormies where we sleep, and our common rooms – the rooms we play about in, you know, when we're not in class," said Darrell. "Our housemistress is Miss Potts. By the way, which tower are you in?"

There was no answer. Darrell looked in angry indignation at Zerelda. She was fast asleep! She hadn't heard a single word of all that Darrell had been telling her! *Well!*

Back at School Again

Darrell was so annoyed with Zerelda for falling asleep whilst she told her all about her beloved Malory Towers that she made up her mind not to say another word when Zerelda deigned to wake up.

She took a good look at the American girl. She was certainly very striking-looking, though her mane of hair was not really a very nice shade of gold. Darrell thought that Brass was a good surname for Zerelda. Her hair did look brassy! Darrell wondered if it had been dyed. But no, surely nobody would let her do that. Perhaps girls grew up more quickly in America though?

"It's a pity she's coming to Malory Towers," thought Darrell, looking closely at Zerelda's beautiful-ly powdered face, with its curling eye-lashes and rosy cheeks. "She just won't fit. Though Gwendoline will

11

love her, I expect! But Gwendoline Mary always does lose her silly heart to people like Zerelda!"

Mr Rivers looked back at the sleeping Zerelda and gave Darrell a comradely grin. She smiled back. She wondered what Zerelda's father and mother could be like; she thought they must be pretty strange to have a daughter like Zerelda.

Then she gave herself a little shake. "She may be quite nice really. It may just be because she comes from a country that lets its girls grow up sooner than ours do," thought Darrell. She was a very fair and just girl and she made up her mind to give Zerelda a chance.

"Though thank goodness she'll be in a higher form, as she's nearly sixteen," thought Darrell. "I shan't see much of her. I hope she's not in North Tower. Oh dear – whatever would Miss Potts think of her if she was!"

She thought of the downright Miss Potts. She thought of plump, sensible Matron who never stood any nonsense from anyone. And she thought of the mistress who took the third form, in which Darrell had already been for a term.

"Miss Peters! Gracious! She'd have a fit if Zerelda was in her form!" thought Darrell, seeing the mannish, hearty-voiced Miss Peters in her mind's eye. "It's really almost a pity she won't be in my form. I'd love to see Miss Peters deal with Zerelda!"

Darrell was tired when they at last reached Malory Towers. They had stopped twice on the way for meals, and Zerelda had awakened, and talked in a gracious, grown-up manner to Mr and Mrs Rivers. Apparently she thought England was "just wunnerful". She also thought that she, Zerelda, could teach it a few things.

Mrs Rivers was polite and friendly, as she always was to everyone. Mr Rivers, who had no patience with people like Zerelda, talked to Darrell and ignored the American girl.

"Say, isn't your father wunnerful?" said Zerelda to Darrell, when they were speeding on their way again. "Those great eyes of his – and the black beetling brows? Wunnerful!"

Darrell wanted to giggle. She longed to tell her father about his "black beetling brows" but there was no chance.

"Tell me about this school of yours," said Zerelda, sweetly, thinking that Darrell was rather silent.

"I've told you already," said Darrell, rather stiffly, "but you must have been bored because you went to sleep."

"Say, isn't that just too bad?" said Zerelda, apologetically.

"There's no time to tell you anything, anyway," said Darrell, "because here we are!" Her eyes shone as they always did when they saw Malory Towers again for the first time.

The car swept up to the front door. It always seemed like the entrance to a castle, to Darrell. The big drive was now crowded with cars, and girls of all ages were rushing about, carrying bags and lacrosse sticks.

"Come on," said Darrell to Zerelda. "Let's get out. Golly, it's grand to be back! Hallo, Belinda! I say, Irene, got your health certificate? Hallo, Jean. Heard about Sally? She's in quarantine. Sickening, isn't it?"

Jean caught sight of Zerelda getting out of the car, and stared as if she couldn't believe her eyes. Zerelda still had no hat on, and her hair cascaded down her

13

shoulders, and the roll on top glinted in a ray of late sunshine.

"Golly – who's that? Some relation of yours?" said Jean.

Darrell giggled. "No, thank goodness. She's a new girl!"

"*No*! My word, what does she think she's come to Malory Towers for? To act in the films?"

Darrell darted here and there among her friends, happy and excited. Her father undid the trunks, and the school porter carried them in. Darrell caught sight of the label on Zerelda's trunk. "North Tower".

"Blow! She's in our tower after all," she thought. "Hallo, Alicia! Had good hols?"

Alicia came up, her bright eyes gleaming. "Super!" she said. "My word – who's that?"

"New girl," said Darrell. "I know how you feel. *I* couldn't take my eyes off her either when I first saw her. Unbelievable, isn't she?"

"Look – there's our dear Gwendoline Mary having a weep on Mother's shoulder as usual!" said Alicia, her attention caught by the sight of Gwendoline's mother, who was dabbing away tears as she said goodbye to Gwendoline.

"There's Miss Winter, Gwendoline's old governess, too," said Darrell. 'No wonder poor Gwen never gets any better – always Mother's Darling Pet. We get some sense into her in term-time, and then she loses it all again in the hols."

Gwendoline caught sight of Zerelda and stared in surprise. A look of great admiration came over her face. Alicia nudged Darrell.

"Gwendoline's going to worship Zerelda, Look! Don't you know that expression on her face? Zerelda will have at least one willing slave!"

Gwendoline said something to her mother and her governess. They both looked at Zerelda. But it was plain that neither of them liked the look of her as much as Gwendoline did.

"Goodbye, darling," said her mother, still dabbing her eyes. "Write to me heaps of times."

But Gwendoline Mary was not paying much attention. She was wondering if anyone was looking after Zerelda. Could she possibly go up to her and offer to show her round? Then she saw that Darrell was with her. Darrell would soon push her off if she went up, she knew.

Zerelda stood looking round at all the bustle and excitement. She was dressed in the same brown coat, brown stockings and shoes as the others, yet she managed to look quite different. She didn't seem to notice the curious glances thrown at her. Darrell, seeing her father and mother about to go, rushed over to them to say goodbye.

"It's so nice to see you plunging into everything so happily as soon as you're back," said her mother, pleased to see how gladly everyone greeted Darrell. "You are no longer one of the smaller ones, Darrell – you seem quite big compared to the first- and second-formers now!"

"I should think so! Babies!" said Darrell, with a laugh. "Goodbye, darlings. I'll write on Sunday as usual. Give Felicity my love and tell her Malory Towers is as nice as ever."

The car moved off down the drive. Darrell waved till it was gone. Then she felt a punch on the back and turned to see Irene there. "Darrell! Come along to Matron with me. I can't find my health certificate."

"Irene! I don't believe you," said Darrell. "Yes, I'll come. Where's my nightcase? Oh, there it is. Hey, Gwendoline, look out with that lacrosse stick of yours. That's twice you've tripped me up."

Darrell suddenly remembered Zerelda. "Oh golly! I've forgotten Zerelda. She's going to be in North Tower too. I'd better get her or she'll be feeling absolutely lost. I know how I felt when I came here first – everyone laughing and ragging and talking and I didn't know a soul!"

She set off towards Zerelda. But Zerelda did not look at all lost or bewildered. She looked thoroughly at home, with a tiny smile on her red mouth as if she was really rather amused by everything going on around her.

Before Darrell could reach her someone else spoke to Zerelda.

"Are you a new girl? I believe you are in North Tower. If you like to come with me I'll show you round a bit."

"Gee, that's kind of you," said Zerelda, in her slow drawl.

"Look," said Darrell, in disgust. "There's Gwendoline Mary all over her already! Trust *her*! She just adores anyone like Zerelda. Zerelda, come with us. We'll take you to Matron."

"I'll look after her, Darrell," said Gwendoline, turning her large pale-blue eyes on Darrell. "You go and look for Sally."

"Sally's not coming back yet," said Darrell, "she's in quarantine. I'll look after Zerelda. She came down with us."

"You can *both* take me around," said Zerelda, charmingly, and smiled her slow smile at Gwendoline.

16

Gwen slipped her arm through Zerelda's and took her up the steps into the hall.

Alicia grinned. "Let's hope dear Gwen will take her off our hands for good," she said. "But I suppose she'll be in a much higher form. She looks about eighteen!"

The groans of Irene attracted their attention. "Oh, Irene! I simply don't believe you've lost your health certificate again," said Darrell. "Nobody could possibly lose it term after term as you do."

"Well, I have," said Irene. "Do come to Matron now and stand by me."

So they all went to find Matron. Darrell and Alicia gave up their health certificates. Matron looked at Irene.

"I've lost it, Matron," said Irene. "The worst of it is I don't even remember having it today! I mean, I usually remember Mother giving it to me, anyhow – but I don't even remember that this time. My memory's getting worse than ever."

"Your mother came to see me not ten minutes ago," said Matron, "and she gave me your certificate herself. Go away, Irene, or you'll make me lose it too!"

Gwendoline brought Zerelda to Matron. Matron stared as if she couldn't believe her eyes. "Who's this? Oh – Zerelda Brass. Yes, you're in North Tower. Is this your health certificate? She's in your dormy, Gwendoline. Take her there – and – er – get her ready to go down for a meal."

Darrell grinned at Alicia, and Alicia winked back. Matron wouldn't be quite so polite about Zerelda tomorrow.

"Come on," said Alicia. "Let's go and unpack our nightcases. I've heaps to tell you, Darrell!"

17

"Any more new girls coming, have you heard?" Darrell asked Alicia.

"Yes, one. Somebody called Wilhelmina," said Alicia. "She's coming tomorrow. One of my brothers knows one of *her* brothers. When he heard she was coming here, he whistled like anything and said, 'Bill will wake you up all right!' "

"Who's Bill?" said Darrell.

"Wilhelmina, apparently," said Alicia, taking the things out of her nightcase. "She's got seven brothers! Imagine it! *Seven*! And she's the only girl."

"Golly!" said Darrell, trying to imagine what it would be like to have seven brothers. She had none. Alicia had three. But seven!

"I should think she's half a boy herself then," said Darrell.

"Probably," said Alicia. "Blow, where's my toothbrush? I know I packed it."

"Look – there's Mavis!" said Darrell. Alicia looked up. Mavis had been a new girl last term. She had not been a great success, because she was lazy and selfish. She had a beautiful voice, pure and sweet, but curiously deep – a most unusual voice that was being well trained.

Mavis was proud of her voice and proud of the career she was going to have. "When I'm an opera-singer," she was always saying, "I shall sing in Milan. I shall sing in New York. When I'm an opera-singer, I shall . . ."

The others got very tired of hearing about Mavis' future career. But they were most impressed with her strong, deep voice, that could easily fill the great school hall. It was so rich and sweet that even the little ones listened in delight.

"But the worst of Mavis is that she thinks she's just perfect because she's got such a lovely voice," Jean had complained a dozen times the term before. Jean was head girl of the third form, and very blunt and forthright. "She doesn't see that she's only just a schoolgirl, with duties to do, and work to get through, and games to play. She's always thinking of that voice of hers – and it's wonderful, we all know that. But what a pity to have a wonderful voice in such a poor sort of person!"

Darrell hadn't liked Mavis. She looked at her now. She saw a discontented, conceited little face, with small dark eyes and a big mouth. Auburn hair was plaited into two thick braids.

"Mavis is all voice and vanity and nothing else," she said to Alicia. "I know that sounds horrid, but it's true."

"Yes," said Alicia, and paused to glance at Mavis too. "And yet, Darrell, that girl will have a wonderful career with that voice of hers, you know. It's unique, and she'll have the whole world at her feet later on. The trouble is that she knows it now."

"I wonder if Gwendoline will still go on fussing round her, now she's seen Zerelda?" said Darrell. Gwendoline, always ready to fawn round anyone gifted, rich or beautiful, had run round Mavis in a ridiculous way the term before. But then Gwendoline Mary never learnt that one should pick one's friends for quite different things. She was quite unable to see why Darrell liked Sally, or why Daphne liked little Mary-Lou, or why everyone liked honest, trustable Jean.

"Where's Betty?" asked Darrell. "I haven't seen her yet." Betty was Alicia's best friend, as clever and amusing as Alicia, and almost as sharp-tongued. She was not in North Tower, much to Alicia's sorrow. But Miss Grayling, the Head Mistress, did not intend to put the two girls into the same house. She was sorry they were friends, because they were too alike, and got each other into trouble continually because of their happy-go-lucky, don't-care ways.

"Betty's not coming back till half-term," said Alicia, gloomily. "She's got whooping-cough. Imagine it – six weeks before she can come back. She's only just started it. I heard yesterday."

"Oh, I say – you'll miss her, won't you?" said Darrell. "I shall miss Sally too."

"Well, we'll just have to put up with each other, you and I, till Betty and Sally come back," said Alicia. Darrell nodded. Alicia amused her. She was always fun to be with, and even when her tongue was sharpest, it was witty. Alicia was lucky. She had such good brains that she could play the fool all she liked and yet not lose her place in class.

"But if *I* do that, I slide down to the bottom at once," thought Darrell. "I've got quite good brains but I've got to use them all the time. Alicia's brains seem to work whether she uses them or not!"

Mary-Lou came up. She had grown a little taller, but she was still the same rather scared-looking girl.

"Hallo!" she said. "Wherever did you pick Zerelda up, Darrell? I hear she came down with you. How old is she? Eighteen?"

"No. Nearly sixteen," said Darrell. "I suppose Gwendoline is sucking up to her already? Isn't she the limit? I say, what do you suppose Miss Potts will say when she sees Zerelda?"

Miss Potts was the house mistress of North Tower, and, like Matron, not very good at putting up with nonsense of any sort. Most of the girls had been in her form, because she taught the bottom class. They liked and respected her. A few girls, such as Gwendoline and Mavis, feared her, because she could be very sarcastic over airs and graces, or pretences of any sort.

Darrell felt rather lost without Sally there to laugh with and talk to. She was glad to walk downstairs with Alicia. Belinda came bouncing up.

"Where's Sally? Darrell, I did some wizard sketching in the hols. I went to the circus, and I've got a whole book of circus sketches. You should just see the clowns!"

"Show the book to us this evening," said Darrell, eagerly. Everyone loved Belinda's clever sketches. She really had a gift for drawing, but, unlike Mavis, she was not forever thinking and talking of it, or of her future career. She was a jolly schoolgirl first and foremost, and an artist second.

"Seen Irene?" said Alicia. Belinda nodded. Irene was her friend, and the two were very well-matched. Irene was talented at music and maths, but a scatter-brain at everything else. Belinda was talented at drawing, quite fair at other lessons, and a scatterbrain almost as bad as Irene. The class had great fun with them.

21

"Seen Zerelda?" asked Darrell, with a grin. That was the question everyone asked that evening. "Seen Zerelda?" No one had ever seen a girl quite like Zerelda before.

At supper that night there was a great noise. Everyone was excited. Mam'zelle Dupont beamed at the table of the third-formers of North Tower.

"You have had good holidays?" she enquired of everyone. "You have been to the theatre and the pantomime and the circus? Ah, you are all ready to work hard now and do some very very good translations for me! *N'est ce pas?*"

There was a groan from the girls round the table. "No, Mam'zelle! Don't let's do French translations this term. We've forgotten all our French!"

Mam'zelle looked round the table for any new face. She always made a point of being extra kind to new girls. She suddenly caught sight of Zerelda and stared in amazement. Zerelda had done her hair again, and her golden roll stood out on top. Her lips were suspiciously red. Her cheeks were far too pink.

"This girl, she is made up for the films!" said Mam'zelle to herself. "Oh, *là là*. Why has she come here? She is not a young girl. She looks old – about twenty! Why has Miss Grayling taken her here? She is not for Malory Towers."

Zerelda seemed quite at home. She ate her supper very composedly. She was sitting next to Gwendoline, who was trying to make her talk. But Zerelda was not like Mavis, willing to talk for hours about herself. She answered Gwendoline politely enough.

"Have you lived all your life in America? Do you think you'll like England?" persisted Gwendoline.

"I think England's just wunnerful," said Zerelda,

22

for the sixth time. "I think your little fields are wunnerful, and your little old houses. I think the English people are wunnerful too."

"Wunnerful, isn't she?" said Alicia, under her breath to Darrell. "Just wunnerful."

Everyone had to go early to bed on the first night, because most of the girls had had long journeys down to Cornwall. In fact, before supper was over there were many loud yawns to be heard.

Zerelda was surprised when Gwendoline informed her that they had to go to bed that night just about eight o'clock. "Only just tonight though," said Gwendoline. "Tomorrow the third-formers go at nine."

"At *nine*," said Zerelda, astonished. "But in my country we go when we like. I shall never go to sleep so early."

"Well, you slept in the car all right," Darrell couldn't help saying. "So you must be tired."

They all went to the common room after supper, chose their lockers, argued, switched on the wireless, switched it off again, yawned, poked the fire, teased Mary-Lou because she jumped when a spark flew out, and then sang a few songs.

Mavis's voice dominated the rest. It really was a most remarkable voice, deep and powerful. It seemed impossible that it should come from Mavis, who was not at all well-grown for her age. One by one the girls fell silent and listened. Mavis sang on. She loved the sound of her own voice.

"Wunnerful!" said Zerelda, clapping loudly when the song was ended. "Ree-markable!"

Mavis looked pleased. "When I'm an opera singer," she began.

Zerelda interrupted her. "Oh, that's what you're

going to be, is it? Gee, that's fine. *I'm* going in for films!"

"Films! What do you mean? A film actress?" said Gwendoline Mary, her eyes wide.

"Yes. I act pretty well already," said Zerelda, not very modestly. "I'm always acting at home. I'm in our Dramatic Society, of course, and last year at College I acted Lady Macbeth in Shakespeare. Gee, that was . . ."

"Wunnerful!" said Alicia, Irene and Belinda all together. Zerelda laughed.

"I guess I don't say things the way you say them," she said, good-naturedly.

"You'll have a chance to show how well you can act, this very term," said Gwendoline, remembering something. "Our form's got to act a play – 'Romeo and Juliet'. You could be Juliet."

"That depends on Miss Hibbert," said Daphne's voice at once. Daphne had already imagined herself in Juliet's part. "Miss Hibbert's our English mistress, Zerelda, and . . ."

"Bed, girls," said Miss Potts' voice at the door. "Eight o'clock! Come along, everyone, or you'll never be up in the morning!"

Zerelda goes into the Fourth

It was fun settling in the next day. The girls rushed into the third-form classroom, which overlooked the courtyard and had a distant view of the sea.

"Zerelda's to go to the fourth-form classroom" said Jean, looking round for the American girl. "She's not with us after all."

"I didn't think I would be," said Zerelda. "I'm much older."

Jean looked at her. "Zerelda," said Jean, "I'd better give you a word of advice. Miss Williams, the fourth form mistress, won't like your hairstyle – or your lipstick either. You'd better alter your hair and rub that awful stuff off your lips before you go to the fourth form. Anyway, they'll rag you like anything if you don't."

"Why should I do what you tell me?" said Zerelda, on her dignity at once. She thought a great deal of her appearance and could not bear to have it remarked on by these proper English girls.

"Well, I'm head girl of this form," said Jean. "That's why I'm bothering to tell you. Just to save you getting into trouble."

"But Zerelda's hair looks lovely," said Gwendoline, who always resented having to have her own hair tied neatly, instead of in a golden sheet over her shoulders.

Nobody took the slightest notice of Gwendoline's bleating.

"Well, thanks all the same, Jean, but I'm not going to make myself into a little pig-tailed English schoolgirl," said Zerelda, in her lazy, rather insolent drawl. "I guess I couldn't look like you, anyway. Look at you all, plain as pie! You ought to let me have a try at making you up – I'd soon get you some looks!"

Daphne, who fancied herself as very pretty, laughed scornfully. "Nobody wants to look a scarecrow like you! Honestly, if you could see yourself!"

"I have," said Zerelda. "I looked in the glass this morning!"

"When you're in Rome, you must do as Rome does," said Jean, solemnly.

"But I'm not in Rome," said Zerelda.

"No. It's a pity you aren't!" said Alicia. "You'll wish you were in three minutes' time when Miss Williams catches sight of you. Go on into the class-room next door for goodness' sake. Miss Williams will be along in half a minute. So will our teacher, Miss Peters. She'd have a blue fit if she saw you."

Zerelda grinned good-humouredly, and went off to find her classroom. As she got to the door Miss Williams came hurrying along to the fourth-formers. She and Zerelda met at the door.

Miss Williams had no idea that Zerelda was one of her form. The girl looked so grown-up. Miss Williams blinked once or twice, trying to remember who Zerelda was. Could she be one of the new assistant mistresses?

"Er – let me see now – you are Miss Miss – er . . . Miss . . ." began Miss Williams.

"Zerelda," said Zerelda, obligingly, thinking it was a strange thing if the mistresses all called the girls "Miss".

"Miss Zerelda," said Miss Williams, still not realizing anything. "Did you want me, Miss Zerelda?"

Zerelda was rather astonished. "Well – er – not exactly," she said. "I was told to come along to your class. I'm in the fourth form."

"Good heavens!" said Miss Williams, weakly. "Not – not one of the girls?"

"Yes, Miss Williams," said Zerelda, thinking that the teacher was acting very strangely. "Say, haven't I

26

done right? Isn't this the classroom?"

"Yes," said Miss Williams, recovering herself all at once. "This is the fourth-form room. But you can't come in like that. What's that thing you've got on the top of your head?"

Zerelda looked even more astonished. Had she got a hat on by mistake? She felt to see. No, there was no hat there.

"There's nothing on my head," she said.

"Yes, there is. What's *this* thing?" said Miss Williams, patting the enormous roll of hair that Zerelda had pinned there in imitation of one of the film stars.

"That? Oh, that's a bit of my hair," said Zerelda, wondering if Miss Williams was a little mad. "It really *is* my hair, Miss Williams. I've just rolled the front part up and pinned it."

Miss Williams looked in silence at the roll of brassy-coloured hair and the cascades of curls down Zerelda's neck. She peered at the too-red lips. She even looked at the curling eyelashes to make sure they were real and not stuck on.

"Well, Zerelda, I can't have you in my class like this," she said, looking very prim and bird-like. "Take down that roll of hair. Tie it all back. Clean your lips. Come back to the room in five minutes."

And with that she disappeared into the form room and the door was shut. Zerelda stared after her. She patted the roll of hair on top. What was the matter with it? Didn't it make her look exactly like Lossie Laxton, the film star she admired most of all?

Zerelda frowned. What a school! Here were a whole lot of girls, all growing up fast, and not one of them knew how to do her hair, not one of them looked smart – "and I bet they're all as stupid as owls," said Zerelda

27

out loud.

She decided to go along and do something to her hair. That prim and proper Miss Williams might say something to the Head. Zerelda had been very much impressed with Miss Grayling and the little talk she had had with her. What had Miss Grayling said? Something about learning to be good-hearted and kind, sensible and trustable, good, sound women the world could lean on. She had also said that Zerelda might learn something from her stay in England that would help her afterwards – and that Zerelda, if she was sensible and understanding, might also teach the English girls something.

"Well, I don't want to get on the wrong side of Miss Grayling from the word go," thought Zerelda, as she went to find her dormy. "Where's this bedroom of ours? I'll never find my way about in this place."

She found the dormy at last and went in to do her hair. She looked at herself in the glass. She was very sad at having to take down that beautiful roll of hair. It took her ages to put it there each morning. But she unpinned it and brushed it out. She divided it into two, and pinned it back, then tied her mane of hair with a piece of ribbon so that it no longer fell wildly over her shoulders.

At once she looked younger. She rubbed the red from her lips. Then she looked at herself. "You look plain and drab now, Zerelda," she said to herself. "What would Pop say? He wouldn't know me!"

But Zerelda didn't look plain and drab. She looked a young girl, with a natural, pleasant youthful face. She went slowly to find her classroom. She was not sure whether she had to knock at the door or not. Things seemed to be so different in an English school

– more polite and proper than in an American school. She decided to knock.

"Come in!" called Miss Williams, impatiently. She had forgotten all about Zerelda. Zerelda went in. She now looked so completely different that Miss Williams didn't recognize her!

"What do you want?" she asked Zerelda. "Have you come with a message?"

"No," said Zerelda, puzzled. "I'm in the fourth form, aren't I?"

"What's your name?" said Miss Williams, looking for her list of names.

Zerelda was now quite certain that Miss Williams was mad. "I told you before," she said. "I'm Zerelda."

"Oh, good gracious – so you are," said Miss Williams, looking at her keenly. "Well, who would have thought your hair would make such a difference! Come and sit down. That's your place over there."

The fourth form were mystified and amused. They were all keen hard-working fifteen-year-olds, who were to work for their School Certificate that year.

"Let me see – how old are you, Zerelda?" said Miss Williams, trying to find Zerelda's name on her list.

"Nearly sixteen," said Zerelda.

"Ah then – you will probably find the work of this form rather easy," said Miss Williams. "But as it's your first term in an English school, that's just as well. There will be many different things for you to learn."

Zerelda looked round at the fourth-formers. She thought they looked too clever for words. How serious they were! She wished she was back in the third form with Alicia, Darrell, Belinda and the rest. They had all seemed so jolly and care-free.

29

The third form were busy making out timetables and lists of duties. Books were given out. Miss Peters, tall, mannish, with very soft hair and a deep voice, was in charge. The girls liked her, but sometimes wished she would not treat them as though they were boys. She had a hearty laugh, and a hearty manner. In the holidays she rode practically all the time, and was in charge of the riding teams on Saturday mornings at Malory Towers.

"I really wonder she doesn't come to class in riding breeches," Alicia had said often enough to the third form, making them giggle. "I'm sure she hates wearing a skirt!"

"Shall I put a set of books for the new girl, Wilhelmina Robinson?" asked Jean, who was in charge of the books. "When is she coming, Miss Peters?"

"This morning, I believe," said Miss Peters. "She and her brothers have been in quarantine for something or other. I think Miss Grayling said she would be arriving this morning. By car, I suppose."

After break the third form went to the sewing room for half an hour, and it was from there that they saw the arrival, the quite astonishing arrival, of Wilhelmina Robinson.

They suddenly heard the clatter of horses' hooves outside − a tremendous clatter. Alicia went to the window at once, wondering if there was a riding lesson for anyone. She gave an exclamation.

"I say! Just look here! Whoever is it?"

All the class crowded to the window. Miss Donnelly, the gentle, sweet-tempered sewing mistress, protested mildly. "Girls, girls! What are you doing?"

"Miss Donnelly, come and look," said Alicia. So

she went to the window. She saw a girl on a big black horse, and with her were seven boys, ranging in age from about eight to eighteen, each of them on horseback! There was a great deal of laughter, and stamping and curveting and cries of "Whoa there!"

"Golly! It must be Wilhelmina!" said Darrell. "And her seven brothers! Don't say that her brothers are coming to Malory Towers too!"

"Well! What a way to arrive!" said Gwendoline Mary. "Galloping up like that on horseback! What a peculiar family Wilhelmina's must be!"

The Arrival of Wilhelmina

Unfortunately the bell for the next class rang at that moment and the third-formers could not see what happened next. Would Miss Grayling come out to the horse riders? How would Wilhelmina enter the Towers? Darrell imagined her riding up the steps and into the hall!

"Golly! Fancy riding to school like that," said Alicia. "I suppose she's going to keep her horse here. One or two girls do do that already. Bringing all her seven brothers too! What a girl!"

Nobody had been able to see clearly what Wilhelmina had looked like. In fact, it had been difficult to tell her from the boys, as they had all been in riding breeches. The third-formers went to their classroom, discussing the new arrival excitedly. Wilhelmina

31

promised to be a Somebody!

"I shall be scared of her," said Mary-Lou.

"Don't be silly," said Mavis, who was always very scornful of Mary-Lou. "Why should you be scared of her? I just hate tomboys, and I'm sure she's one. She'll think of nothing but horses and dogs, and she'll smell of them too. People always do when they're mad on animals."

"Miss Peters doesn't," said Darrell.

"Oh, Miss Peters!" said Mavis. "I'll be glad when I'm out of her class. She's too hearty for anything!"

Darrell laughed. Miss Peters was rather hearty and loud-voiced. But she was a good sort, though not at all sympathetic to people like Mavis. Neither had she much patience with Alicia or Betty when they played any of their idiotic tricks. In fact, she had looked with such disfavour on tricks in class that poor Alicia and Betty had almost given up playing any.

Wilhelmina didn't turn up in the classroom that morning, but Jean found Matron waiting for her in the passasge when the third form went out to get ready for dinner. With her was somebody who, except for the school tunic, looked exactly like a boy!

"Jean," said Matron, "you're head girl of the third, aren't you? Well, look after Wilhelmina for me, will you, and take her down to dinner? She couldn't come yesterday because she wasn't out of quarantine. Here you are, Wilhelmina – this is Jean, head girl of your form."

"Hallo," said Wilhelmina and grinned a boyish grin that showed big white teeth set very evenly. Jean looked at her and liked her at once.

Wilhelmina had hair cropped almost as short as a boy's. It curled a little, which she hated. Her face was boyish and square, with a tip-tilted nose, a big mouth, and big, wide-set eyes of hazel-brown. She was covered with freckles from forehead to firm little chin.

"Hallo," said Jean. "I saw you arrive – on horse-back, didn't you?"

"Yes," said Wilhelmina. "My seven brothers came with me. Mummy was awfully cross about that. She wanted me to go in the car with her and Daddy – but we got our horses and shot off before they started!"

"Good gracious!" said Jean. "Did you really? Have you each got a horse?"

"Yes. We've got big stables," said Wilhelmina. "Daddy keeps racehorses too. I say – I've never been to boarding school before. Is it awful? If it is I shall saddle Thunder and ride away."

Jean stared at Wilhelmina and wondered if she meant all this. She decided that she didn't. She laughed and pulled Wilhelmina along to the cloak-room, because she had to wash ink off her hands before dinner. Miss Potts would be sure to spot them if she didn't!

"Malory Towers is a jolly fine school," said Jean. "You'll like it."

"Shall I be able to ride Thunder each day?" asked Wilhelmina, staring round the big cloakroom where girls were chattering and laughing as they washed. "I tell you, I wouldn't have come if they hadn't let me bring Thunder. I shall have to look after him too, even if it means missing some of my lessons. He would hate anyone else looking after him."

"Haven't you ever been to school before?" asked Belinda, who had been listening to all this with interest.

"No. I shared the tutor that three of my brothers

33

had," said Wilhelmina. "There wasn't a school near at all. We live miles out in the country. I expect I shall be at the bottom of the form."

Belinda liked this outspoken girl. "I bet you won't," she said, and cast her eye round to see if Gwendoline was about. Yes, she was. "Not while Gwendoline Mary is in the form, anyway!"

"Don't be beastly," said Gwendoline, cross at having fun poked at her in front of a new girl.

"It will all seem a bit strange to you at first," said Jean. "If you've been even to a day school before it helps – but never to have been to school at all – well, you're sure to feel a bit strange, Wilhelmina."

"I say – would you mind very much if I asked you something?" said Wilhelmina, staring hard at Jean.

"What?" said Jean, wondering what was coming. The others came round to listen. Wilhelmina looked round at them all.

"Well," she said, "I've never in my life been called Wilhelmina. Never. It's a frightful name. Everyone calls me Bill. After all, people call William Bill for short, don't they? So my brothers said they'd call me Bill, short for Wilhelmina! If you all start calling me Wilhelmina I shall be miserable. I shan't feel I'm myself."

In the usual way if a new girl asked for a nickname, she would have been laughed at, or told to think again. Nicknames were only given when people knew you well and liked you. Gwendoline Mary opened her mouth to say this but Belinda spoke first.

"Yes. We'll call you Bill. It suits you. Wilhelmina's a nice name for some people, but not for you. You really *are* a Bill. What do you say, Darrell – and Jean?"

"Yes," they agreed at once. They couldn't help

liking this sturdy, freckled girl with her short hair and frank smile. She *was* Bill. They couldn't possibly call her anything else.

"Well, thanks awfully," said Bill. "Thanks *most* awfully. Now I can forget I was ever christened Wilhelmina."

Mavis and Gwendoline Mary looked as if they didn't approve of this at all. Why should a new girl get a nickname at once, just because she wanted it? Daphne looked disapproving too. How could any girl want a boy's name? And how could anyone wear her hair as short as Wilhelmina and get so many freckles? Why, Daphne couldn't bear it if she got so much as a single freckle!

Zerelda came into the cloakroom, her hair still done properly, without the big roll on top of her head. Jean looked at her.

"Gracious, Zerelda! You do look different – about ten years younger! I bet Miss Williams was mad with you, wasn't she?"

"She was mad all right," said Zerelda. "Really mad, I mean! I'm quite scared of her. I'd rather have your Miss Peters. I say – who in the big wide world is this?"

She stood and stared in the utmost wonder at Bill, who looked back, quite unabashed. The two took in one another from top to toe.

"Are you a boy or a girl?" inquired Zerelda. "Gee, I wouldn't know!"

"My name's Bill," said Bill with a grin. "Short for Wilhelmina. What's yours?"

"Zerelda. Short for nothing," said Zerelda. "Why do you wear your hair like that?"

"Because I couldn't bear to wear it like yours," retorted Bill.

35

Zerelda stared at Bill again as if she really couldn't believe her eyes.

"I've never seen a girl like you before," she said. "Gee, you're wunnerful! Gee, I think all you English people are wunnerful!"

"Anyone would think you hadn't got an English mother," said Darrell. "You've lived with her all your life, haven't you? You always sound as if you have never met anyone English before."

"My mother's as American as anyone," said Zerelda. "I don't know why she's gotten it into her head to send me to England. She's forgotten she was ever English. I'd like to take you back to America with me, Bill. Why, nobody would believe you were real, over there! Gee, you're just . . ."

"WUNNERFUL!" chorused everyone, and Zerelda laughed.

A bell rang. "Dinner!" yelled Belinda. "I'm starving. Rotten breakfasts we get here!"

"Rotten!" agreed everyone. They had all eaten big plates of porridge and milk, scrambled eggs, and toast and marmalade, but it was always agreed that the food was "rotten" – unless, of course, an outsider dared to criticize the food, and then it suddenly became "too wizard for words."

They tore down to the dining room. Zerelda went to sit with the third-formers, having put up rather a poor show in the fourth form that morning, and feeling rather small — but Miss Williams called her over.

"Zerelda! This is your table now. Let me look at your hair."

Zerelda submitted to Miss Williams' close examination, glad that she had not put any red on her lips. How dare Miss Williams treat her like a kid of six? She felt angry and annoyed. But she soon cheered up when she saw the steaming dishes of stew, surrounded with all kinds of vegetables. Gee, she liked these English meals. They were – no, not wunnerful – what was the word the others used – yes, they were wizard!

Darrell wrote to Sally that night and told her about Bill and Zerelda.

You'll like Bill (short for Wilhelmina), [*she wrote*]. All grins and freckles and very short hair, mad on horses, has seven brothers, says just exactly what she thinks, and yet we don't mind a bit.

She bit her pen and then went on.

But, oh my, *Zerelda*! She thinks she's going to be a film star and says she's "wunnerful" at acting. You should have seen the way she did her hair – and the way she made up her face! We thought we were going to have some fun with her and take her down a peg or two, but she's not in our form after all. She's nearly sixteen so she's gone into the fourth. I bet Miss Williams had a fit when she saw her walking into her classroom this morning. Sally, do hurry up and come back. Betty isn't back yet either, so Alicia and I are keeping each other company, but I'd so *much* rather have you. You steady me! Alicia doesn't. She makes me feel I'm going to do idiotic things. I hope I'll last out till you·come back!

Somebody put their head in the door. "Hey is Wilhelmina here? Matron wants her. Wilhelmina!"

Nobody stirred. "Wilhelmina!" said the voice again. "Hey, you, new girl! Aren't you Wilhelmina?"

Bill put down her book hastily. "Golly, yes, so I am!" she said. "I quite forgot. I really must tell Matron to call me Bill."

She went out and everyone laughed. "Good old Bill! I'd like to see Matron's face when she tells her to call her Bill!" said Belinda.

Bill and Thunder

After a few days it seemed to Darrell as if she had been back at school for weeks. The world of home seemed very far away. She thought pityingly of her sister Felicity at her day school. Why, Felicity didn't even *guess* what it was like to be at a proper boarding school, where you got up all together, had meals together, planned fun for every evening, and then all rushed off to bed together.

Wilhelmina, or Bill, had been rather silent those first two or three days. Darrell wondered if she was homesick. As a rule the happy, normal girls did not mope and pine – life was so full and so jolly at Malory Towers that there simply wasn't time for anything of that sort.

All the same, she thought Bill looked a bit serious. "Not homesick, are you?" she asked, one morning when she was walking down one of the corridors with Bill.

"Oh no. I'm horse-sick!" said Bill, surprisingly. "I

keep on and on thinking of all our horses at home that I love so much – Beauty and Star and Blackie and Velvet and Midnight and Miss Muffett and Ladybird and . . ."

"Good gracious! However do you remember all those names?" said Darrell, in surprise.

"I couldn't possibly forget them," said Bill solemnly. "I'm going to like Malory Towers, I know that, but I simply can't help missing all our horses, and the thunder of their hooves and the way they neigh and nuzzle – oh, you can't understand, Darrell. You'll think me silly, I know. You see, I and three of my brothers used to ride each morning to our tutor – four miles away – and we used to go out and saddle and bridle our horses – and then off we'd go, galloping over the hills."

"Well, you couldn't do that all your life long," said Darrell, sensibly. "And anyway, you'll do it in the hols again. You're lucky to have been able to bring Thunder with you here."

"That's why I said I'd come to Malory Towers," said Bill. "Because I could bring Thunder. Oh dear, Darrell – it's been the weekend so far, when there weren't lessons – I'm just dreading to think what will happen when I have to go to classes and perhaps shan't see Thunder all day long. It's a pity Miss Peters wouldn't let him stand at the back of the classroom. He'd be as good as gold."

Darrell gave a squeal of laughter. "Oh, Bill – you're mad! Golly, I'd love to have Thunder in the classroom too. I bet he'd neigh at Mam'zelle, and she'd teach him to whinny in French!"

"She wouldn't. She doesn't like horses. She told me so," said Bill. "She's scared of them. Imagine that,

Darrell! I shouldn't have thought there was anyone in the world silly enough to be frightened of a horse."

Most of the third-formers had been out to the stables to see Bill's wonderful horse. Actually he didn't seem very wonderful to Darrell, who didn't know a great deal about horses, but she did think he was lovely the way he welcomed Bill, whinnying in delight, pushing his big velvety nose into the crook of her arm, and showing her as plainly as possible that he adored every bit of his freckled little mistress.

Mavis, Gwendoline, Daphne and Mary-Lou would not go near him. He was a big black horse, and they all felt certain he would kick or bite. But the others loved him.

Zerelda was not scared of him, and she admired him very much. "Gee, he's wunnerful," she said. "But what a pity you've got to get yourself up in those awful breeches to ride him, Wilhelmina."

Bill scowled. She hated to be called by her full name. "I suppose you'd ride him in flowing skirts, with your hair down to your waist – and rings on your fingers and bells on your toes!" she retorted. "All the way to Banbury Cross."

Zerelda didn't understand. She didn't know the old English nursery rhyme. She smiled her lazy smile at Bill.

"You're wunnerful when you scowl like that," she said.

"Shut up," said Bill, and turned away. She was puzzled by Zerelda and her grown-up ways – and even more puzzled by her good humour. Zerelda never seemed to take offence, no matter how much anyone laughed at her or even jeered, as Mavis did very often.

She made the others feel small and young and rather

40

stupid. They felt uncomfortable with her. She really did seem years older, and she deliberately used a grown-up manner, jeering gently at their clothes, their "hairdos" as she called them, their liking for getting hot and muddy at games, and their complete lack of interest in the lives and careers of film stars.

But she was generous and kind, and never lost her temper, so it was difficult really to dislike her. Gwendoline, of course, adored her. She quite neglected Mavis for Zerelda, which annoyed that conceited young opera singer immensely.

The first full week of school began on the next day, Monday. No more leniency from the mistresses, no more slacking from the girls, no more easy-going ways. "Work, now, work for everyone!" said Miss Peters. "It's not a very long term but you must work hard and show good results even if we are a week or two short."

The third form did not have only the third-form girls from North Tower but the third-formers from other towers too, so it was a fairly big form. The standard was high, and Miss Peters was strict.

Mavis had been in Miss Peters' black books the term before, because of her poor work. But as it had been her first term, she had not been too hard on her. But now she, like everyone else, was getting tired of Mavis's parrot-cry, "when I'm an opera singer" and she was quite determined to make Mavis a good third-former, opera singer or not.

"You'd better look out, Mavis," said Gwendoline, catching a certain look in Miss Peters' eye that morning as she studied Mavis. "I know that look! You'll have to work this term, and forget your voice for a bit!"

"When I want your advice I'll ask for it," said Mavis. "I'm not scared of our hearty Miss Peters, if you are! I'm not going to slave and make myself miserable at Malory Towers for miss P. or anyone else. Waste *your* time, if you like – you'll never have a career, or be Somebody!"

Gwendoline was very hurt. Like many silly, weak people she had a great idea of herself, and was so continually spoilt at home that she really did think herself wonderful.

"If you're going to say things like that I shan't be friends with you," she whispered.

"Go and tag round Zerelda then," said Mavis, forgetting to whisper softly enough.

"Mavis! That's enough whispering between you and Gwendoline," said Miss Peters' loud voice. "One more whisper and you can stay in at break."

Bill couldn't seem to settle down that first Monday morning at all. She stared out of the window. She seemed very far away. She paid no attention at all to what Miss Peters was saying.

"Wilhelmina!" said Miss Peters at last. "Did you hear *any*thing of what I have just said?"

Everyone turned to look at Bill, who still gazed out of the window, a dreamy expression on her small square face.

"*Wilhelmina!*" said Miss Peters, sharply. "I am speaking to you."

Still Bill took no notice at all. To the girls' amusement and surprise she suddenly made a little crooning noise, as if she was quite by herself and there was nobody else in the room at all!

Miss Peters was astonished. The girls giggled. Darrell knew what Bill was doing. She had heard that funny little crooning noise before – it was the noise Bill made to Thunder, when he nuzzled against her shoulder!

"She must be pretending she's with Thunder!" thought Darrell. "She's in the stables with him. She's not here at all."

Miss Peters wondered if Wilhelmina was feeling all right. She spoke to her again. "Wilhelmina, are you deaf? What's the matter?"

Gwendoline gave Bill a poke in the back and made her jump. She looked round at Gwendoline crossly, annoyed at being so rudely awakened from her pleasant daydreams. Gwendoline nodded violently towards Miss Peters.

"That'll do, Gwendoline," said Miss Peters. "Wilhelmina, will you kindly give me your attention. I've been speaking to you for the last few minutes."

"Oh, sorry! Have you really?" said Bill, apologetically. "Perhaps you kept calling me Wilhelmina, though? If you could call me Bill I should always answer. You see . . ."

Miss Peters looked most disapproving. What an extraordinary girl!

"In future, Wilhelmina, please pay attention to all I say, and I shall not need to address you by any name at all!" she said. "As for calling you Bill – please don't be impertinent."

Bill looked astonished. "Oh, Miss Peters! I wasn't being impertinent. I'm sorry I wasn't listening to you. I was thinking about Thunder."

"Thunder!" said Miss Peters, who had no idea that Bill had a horse called Thunder. "Why should you think about thunder on a lovely sunny day like this? I think you are being silly."

"But it's just the *day* to think of Thunder!" said Bill, her eyes shining. "Just think of Thunder, galloping over the hills and . . ."

Everyone tried to suppress giggles. They knew perfectly well that Wilhelmina was talking about her horse, but poor miss Peters looked more impatient than ever.

"That's enough, Wilhelmina," she said. "We'll have no more talk of thunder or lightning, or . . ."

"Oh, how did you know that my brother George's horse was called Lightning?" said Bill in delight, honestly thinking that Miss Peters was talking about horses.

But now Miss Peters felt certain that Wilhelmina was being silly and rather rude. She gazed at her coldly.

"Have you got your book open at page thirty-three?" she asked. "I thought you hadn't! How do you think you are going to follow this lesson if you haven't even got the right page?"

Bill hastily found page thirty-three. She tried to put all thoughts of Thunder out of her mind. She made a soft clicking noise, and Alicia and Irene grinned at one another.

"Horse-mad!" whispered Alicia, and when Miss Peters' back was turned, Alicia rocked to and fro as if she was on a trotting horse, sending the class into fits.

Darrell hugged herself in delight. It was lovely to be back at school again, lovely to sit in class and work, and giggle and hear Miss Peters ticking off this person and that. She missed Sally very much, but Alicia was fun.

"I'll beg her to play one of her tricks," thought Darrell. "We haven't had any *real* fun in class for terms and terms!"

44

In The Third-Form Common Room

It was sunny but cold the first week or two of that Easter term. The girls squabbled over getting the seats by the radiator in the common room. Gwendoline, Mavis and Daphne were the ones that complained most of the cold – but they were the ones who took as little exercise as they could, so of course they always got chilblains and colds.

Bill didn't seem to feel the cold at all. She was still tanned, although it was early in the year. Darrell and Alicia liked the cold, and they loved rushing out to play lacrosse in the afternoons.

They went out ten minutes before the others to practise catching. Gwendoline couldn't understand it, and she and Mavis soon became friends again in sympathizing with each other over the cold, and jeering at Alicia and Darrell for being so hardy.

Zerelda, of course, being a fourth-former, was now not very often able to be with any of the third-formers, so Gwendoline had had to give up any idea of being her best friend. Zerelda did not seem to be very happy in the fourth form, Darrell thought. She often came slipping into the third form common room in the evening – saying she wanted to borrow a book or a gramophone record – and then stopping to talk to Darrell and the others.

"Got a special friend yet?" Darrell asked her one evening.

Zerelda twisted one of her curls carefully round her finger and then shook it back into its proper place.

"No," she said. "Stuck-up things, the fourth form! They seem to think I don't pull my weight. And they think the end of the world has come because I don't want to try and get into the third match-team for lacrosse!"

"Well, you're so tall, you could do well in the team," said Darrell, considering her. "You ought to be able to take some fine catches. Can you run?"

"Run! I don't *want* to run!" said Zerelda, astonished. "As for that games captain – what's her name – Molly Ronaldson – well, I ask you, did you ever see such a girl? Big as a horse and just about as clumsy! Shouts and dances about on the field as if she had gone mad!"

Darrell laughed. "Molly Ronaldson is one of the finest games captains we've ever had. We've won more matches with her than ever before. She's got an absolute genius for picking the right people for the match-teams. My goodness, if I could get into one of the teams I'd be so thrilled I wouldn't be able to sleep at night."

"Is that so?" said Zerelda, in her slow drawl, looking quite astonished. "Well, maybe I wouldn't sleep at night if I had spots on my face like Gwendoline goes in for, or if I broke one of my nails – but I'd not lose my beauty sleep for any game in the world!"

"You're a strange person, Zerelda," said Darrell. She looked at her earnestly. "You're missing all the nicest years of your life – I mean, you just won't let yourself enjoy the things most English girls of your age

46

enjoy. You spend hours over your hair and your face and your nails, when you could be having fun at lacrosse, or going for walks, or even messing about in the gym."

"Messing about in the gym! That's another thing I can't understand your liking!" said Zerelda. Gwendoline, who had come up to join in the conversation, nodded her head in agreement.

"I can't understand that either," she said in a prim voice. "It's a pity gym is compulsory, and games too. *I* wouldn't bother much about them if they weren't."

"Only because, dear Gwendoline, you're so jolly bad at them that you make a fool of yourself every time you go into the gym or on the games field," said Alicia, maliciously. "Zerelda's different. I bet she'd be good at them – but she thinks that all that kind of thing is beneath her."

Any other girl would have resented this, but Zerelda only grinned. Gwendoline, however, flared up at the unkind sneer at *her* games and gym performances, and scowled angrily at Alicia.

"Nice little scowl you've got, Gwen," said Belinda, appearing suddenly with her sketchbook. "Do you mind if I draw you like that? It's such a *lovely* scowl!"

Gwendoline scowled still more and flounced away. She knew Belinda's clever pencil and dreaded it! She didn't want her scowl drawn and passed round the common room, accompanied by delighted giggles. Belinda shut her book and looked disappointed in rather an exaggerated manner.

"Oh, she's gone! And it was such a lovely scowl! Never mind – I'll watch out for it and draw it another time."

"Beast!" said Gwendoline, under her breath and

47

went to sit by Mavis. She knew she would have to look out for Belinda and her pencil now! Once Belinda wanted to draw something she didn't rest till she had done so!

"You'd better go back to the fourth-form common room now," said Jean to Zerelda. "The fourth-formers won't like it if you begin to live with us! We're rather beneath their notice, you know. And, after all, you *are* a fourth-former, Zerelda."

"I know. I wish I wasn't," said Zerelda, getting up.

"Aren't the fourth form girls 'wunnerful' then?" said Alicia with a grin.

Zerelda shrugged her shoulders and went out gracefully. "If she'd think of something else besides her looks and the way she's going to act, and being grown-up, and would put herself out to play games decently and take some interest in her work, the fourth form wouldn't make her feel out of things," said Jean, with her usual common sense. "But what's the good of telling Zerelda that? She simply doesn't belong to the school at all."

Irene drifted in, looking for something. She hummed a lively little tune. "Tumty-ta-ti-tumty-ta-ti-too!" She had just composed a jolly dance, and was very pleased about it. The girls looked at her and grinned at one another.

"Where are you off to at this time of the evening, Irene?" asked Alicia.

Irene looked surprised. "Nowhere," she said. "I'm just looking for my music book. I want to write down my new tune. Tumty-ta-ti-tumty-ta-ti-too!"

"Yes, very nice," said Alicia approvingly. "But why have you got your hat and cloak on if you aren't going anywhere?"

"Oh, good gracious, have I?" said Irene, in dismay. She looked down at her cloak and felt her hat on her head. "Blow! When did I put these on? I did take them off, didn't I, when we came back from the walk this afternoon?"

"Well, you didn't have them on at teatime or Miss Potts would have said something!" said Alicia. "You really are a chump, Irene."

"Oh, yes, I know now what must have happened," said Irene, sitting down in a chair, still with hat and cloak on. "I went up to get a clean pair of stockings – and I was thinking of my new tune – and I must have taken my hat out instead of my stockings, and put it on – and then put on my cloak too. Blow! Now I shall have to go and take them off and find my stockings – and I do want to write down that tune."

"I'll take them up for you and find your stockings," said Belinda, who knew that Irene wouldn't be able to do anything sensible till she had written down her tune.

"*Will* you? Angel!" said Irene, and pulled off her hat and cloak. Darrell laughed. Belinda was as much of a scatterbrain as Irene. It would be a wonder if she got as far as the cupboard to put away Irene's things – and ten to one that she wouldn't remember the stockings!

Belinda disappeared with the hat and cloak. Irene began to hum her tune again. Mavis sang it in her lovely rich voice.

"Fine!" said Irene, pleased. "You make it sound twice as good, Mavis. One day I'll write a song for that voice of yours."

"I'll sing it in New York," said Mavis, graciously. "And that should make you famous, Irene, if *I* sing one of your songs! When I'm an opera singer, I . . ."

"When you're an opera singer, Mavis, you'll be even more conceited than you are now," said Alicia's sharp voice, "which sounds impossible I know, but isn't."

"Jean! Can't you stop Alicia saying such beastly unfair things?" protested Mavis, red with annoyance. "I'm *not* conceited. Can I help having a voice like mine? It's a gift, and I shall make it a gift to the whole world too, when I'm grown up."

"Alicia's tongue *is* getting a little sharp," said Jean, "but you do rather ask for sharp things to be said to you, Mavis."

Mavis was silent and cross. Gwendoline began to sympathize with her, for she too hated Alicia's hard hitting. Mary-Lou, darning a stocking in a corner, hoped that she would not come in for a flick of Alicia's tongue!

"Where's Belinda?" said Darrell. "She's an awful long time getting those stockings for you, Irene."

"So she is," said Irene, who had now completely forgotten about the stockings. "Blow! If she doesn't bring them soon, I'll have to go and fetch them myself. I simply must put a clean pair on for supper."

Mam'zelle came bustling in, tip-tapping on her small feet in their high-heeled shoes. She held a hat and cloak in her hand.

"Irene!" she said, reproachfully, "these are yours! Three times already have I cleared up your things from this place and that place. Now this time I have almost fallen down the stairs because of your hat and cloak!"

Irene stared in surprise. "But – where were they?" she asked.

50

"On the stairs – lying for me to fall over," said Mam'zelle. "I see them on the stairs as I come down, and I say to myself, 'What is this? Is is someone taken ill on the stairs!' But no, it is Irene's cloak and hat once more. I am very displeased with you, Irene. You will take an order-mark!"

"Oh *no*, Mam'zelle!" said Irene, distressed. Order-marks counted against the whole form. "Mam'zelle I'm really very sorry."

"One order-mark," said Mam'zelle, and departed on her high heels.

"Blow Belinda!" said Irene. "What possessed her to put them on the stairs?"

Belinda came in at that moment. She was greeted by a volley of remarks. "We've got an order-mark because of you, idiot! What did you do with Irene's things? Mam'zelle found them on the stairs!"

"Golly!" said Belinda, dismayed. "Yes, I remember. I was going up the stairs with them, and I dropped my pencil. I chucked the things down to find it – and must have forgotten all about them. I *am* sorry, Irene."

"It's all right," said Irene, solemnly putting on her hat and cloak. "I'll take them up myself now – and I'll jolly well *wear* them so that *I* can't leave them lying about either!"

She disappeared for a long time. The bell rang for supper. There was a general clearing-up, and the girls got ready to go to the dining room.

"Where's Irene now?" said Jean, exasperated. "Honestly she ought to be kept in a cage then we'd always know where she was!"

"Here she is!" said Darrell, with a shout of laughter. "Irene! You've still got your hat and cloak on! Oh, you'll make us die of laughing. Quick, Alicia, take them off her and rush upstairs with them. She'll get another order-mark if we don't look out."

A Bad Time For Zerelda

During the first two or three weeks of term poor Zerelda had a very bad time. Although she was older even than the fourth-formers, and should therefore have found the work easy, she found, to her dismay, that she was far behind them in their standard of work.

It was a blow to Zerelda. After all her posing, and grown-up ways, and her manner of appearing to look down on the others as young and silly, it was very humiliating to find that her maths, for instance, was nowhere near the standard of maths in the fourth form!

"Have you never done these sums before?" asked Miss Williams, in astonishment. "And what about algebra and geometry? You don't appear to understand the first thing about them, Zerelda."

"We – we don't seem to do our lessons in America the same way as you do them here," said Zerelda. "We don't bother so much. I never liked algebra or geometry, so I didn't worry about them."

Miss Williams looked most disapproving. Was America really so slack in its teaching of children, or was it just that Zerelda was stupid?

"It isn't only our maths," she said at last. "It's

almost everything, Zerelda. Didn't you ever study grammar in your school?"

Zerelda thought hard. "Maybe we did," she said at last. "But I guess we didn't pay much attention to the teacher who taught grammar. I guess we played about in her lessons."

"And didn't you do any history?" said Miss Williams. "I realize, of course, that the history you would take would not be quite the same as ours – but Miss Carton, the history mistress, tells me that you don't know a single thing even about the history of your *own* country. America is a great country. It seems a pity to know nothing of its wonderful history."

Zerelda looked troubled. She tried to think of something her school had really worked at. What had she taken real interest in? Ah – there was the dramatic class!

"We did a lot of Shakespeare, Miss Williams," she said. "Gee! I just loved your Shakespeare. He's wunnerful. I did Lady Macbeth. You should have seen me trying to wash the guilt off my hands."

"Yes. I can quite imagine it," said Miss Williams, dryly. "But there's a little more to education than being able to act Lady Macbeth. Zerelda, you will have to work very very hard to catch up the work of your form. I am willing to give you extra coaching, if you would like it, and Mam'zelle, who is very distressed at your French, says she also will give you some of her free time."

Zerelda was really alarmed. Gee, wasn't it enough to have all these classes and games, and be expected to attend each one and be serious over the work, without having to do a whole lot of extra study? She looked so very alarmed that Miss Williams laughed.

"Well, Zerelda, I won't burden you with extra work just yet, if you'll really make an effort and try to give your attention to your school work and not – er – *quite* so much attention to your face, shall we say – and nails – and hair?"

Zerelda was annoyed. She was going to study to be a famous film star, so what was the use of all this algebra and history stuff? Just waste of time for a girl like her! She had good brains, she knew she had – it was just that American schools and English were so different. They had different standards. Life was easier in America.

She looked down at her long, beautifully polished nails and well-kept hands. She felt that Miss Williams had shamed her and made her feel small. Zerelda couldn't bear that! She was better than any of these tough little English girls any day! They didn't know a thing really!

So she looked stubborn and said nothing. Miss Williams gathered up her papers, thinking that Zerelda was really a very difficult girl.

"Well, that's all for now," she said, briskly. "I shall expect much better work from now on, Zerelda – and please do think of the other fourth-formers too. You know that returned work means an order-mark, which counts against the whole form. You have got far too many."

Zerelda thought that order-marks were very silly. She wouldn't have minded at all getting twenty or thirty a week! But the other fourth-formers minded very much.

The head girl, Lucy, spoke to Zerelda about it. "Look here, Zerelda, can't you stop getting order-marks? There are two half-holidays given this term,

54

but any form getting over forty order-marks has the holiday withheld. The form will be pretty wild if you make them miss their half-holiday, I can tell you!"

So, what with some serious talks from Miss Williams and some tickings-off from Lucy, and from Ellen, a serious, scholarship girl who had gone up from the third form into the fourth, and was very pleased about it, poor Zerelda had rather a bad time.

"There doesn't seem time to do anything!" she thought to herself as she polished her nails that night. "I simply must take care of my hair – and it takes ages to curl it properly and set it – and I can't let my complexion go – or my nails. I don't have a minute to myself. But I simply must do something about the work! I can't bear these English girls to be so much better at everything than I am!"

So Zerelda really did try with the work. But her pride would not let her cast off her posing and her grown-up ways. She no longer really looked down on the English girls, but she was still going to show them that she, Zerelda, was far, far above them in all the ways that mattered!

Zerelda had hoped that she would be able to show her ability for acting in the play the fourth form were going to perform. But, alas! for her, it was a French play, and Zerelda's French did not please Mam'zelle at all.

"*C'est terrible!*" cried Mam'zelle Dupont, and the other Mam'zelle for once agreed with her. Both of them were astonished at Zerelda and her ways, and spent a few pleasant half-hours telling each other of "Zerelda, *cet enfant terrible*," that terrible girl.

When Zerelda had been awarded fifteen order-marks, had three lessons out of every six returned, and

55

had one day given in no prep at all because she said she couldn't do any of it, Miss Williams went to Miss Grayling.

"Zerelda Brass isn't up to the fourth form," she told Miss Grayling. "She's making them furious because of the order-marks she's getting. The trouble is they know what a lot of time she wastes over her appearance, and they think if she gave a bit more time to her work, it would be better all round. I've told her this myself, of course. I don't think she's a bad girl at all, Miss Grayling – only silly, and brought up with quite the wrong ideas. What are we to do?"

"Do you think extra coaching would help?" asked Miss Grayling. "She is nearly sixteen, you know. She ought to be well up to School Certificate standard. She had quite a good report from America."

"No. I don't think extra coaching would help at all," said Miss Williams. "It would worry her too much. She simply isn't up to the fourth form – and I really doubt if she's up to third-form standard either! The trouble is she's got such a great opinion of herself, and appears to look down on the others. They resent it."

"Of course they do," said Miss Grayling. "And quite rightly." She said nothing for a minute. She felt a little disappointed. She had hoped that the American girl would be good for the English girls, and that the English girls would help the American. But apparently it hadn't worked out that way.

"She must go down into the third form," said Miss Grayling at last. "I know it is a humiliation and that Zerelda will feel it a disgrace – but somehow I feel that won't do her any harm. Send her to me."

"Thank you, Miss Grayling," said Miss Williams,

and went out, really relieved to think that Zerelda would no longer be her responsibility. She would now erase all those order-marks that Zerelda had unfortunately got for her form. They would be pleased. They were a good hard-working form, and Miss Williams was proud of them. She was glad to get rid of a girl who had brought them nothing but disgrace.

"But she's not really a *bad* girl," thought Miss Williams, who was very fair-minded. "She's just not up to standard in any way. She'll be better in the third form."

She sent Zerelda down to Miss Grayling. Zerelda, who would have laughed at the thought of being scared of any teacher when she first came to Malory Towers, actually found her heart thumping away hard as she went to find Miss Grayling in her pleasant drawing room.

She went in and stood in front of the Head Mistress' desk. Miss Grayling put down her pen and looked at Zerelda, noting her brassy golden hair, done more neatly now, but still carefully set, her brilliantly polished nails, her carefully powdered face.

"Zerelda, I have sent for you because I think you are not up to the standard of the work in the fourth form," said Miss Grayling, going straight to the point, as she always did. Zerelda flushed bright red.

"I am sorry about this because you are really above their average age," said Miss Grayling. "But I think that it will be too difficult for you to cope with extra work, and also I am afraid that the fourth form, which is a School Certificate form, will not take kindly to quite so many order-marks as you have been producing for them."

Zerelda blushed an even brighter scarlet, and was

57

angry to feel herself going so red. What did she care about the silly fourth form?

"Therefore I think you will do better if you go into the third form," said Miss Grayling. "They don't take life – or lessons – quite so seriously as they will when in the fourth form – so you should be happier there, and able to work better."

Zerelda was shocked. To go down into a lower form! What a disgrace! True, she liked the third-formers, and didn't get on with the fourth form girls – but she didn't want to slide down a whole form! Whatever would her people say – and her English grandmother would be amazed.

"Oh, Miss Grayling – gee, I wouldn't like that," said Zerelda, in distress. She undid a button and did it up again, then undid it, not knowing what she did.

"Don't pull that button off, Zerelda," said Miss Grayling. "I think you'll soon settle down quite well in the third form. You can go there tomorrow. I will tell Miss Peters. Move all your things tonight."

"But, Miss Grayling – don't make me do that!" begged Zerelda, feeling very small and disgraced, and not liking it at all. "This is all new to me, this English school – and the work too. You see . . ."

"Yes, I quite see all that," said Miss Grayling. "It's partly because of that that I think life would be easier for you in the way of work, if you go into a lower form. I am convinced you will not get on at all in a higher form. But, Zerelda – don't slide down any further, will you? You belong to a great country, and you are her only representative here. Be a good one if you can. And I think you can."

This was the one thing that could touch Zerelda. Gee, she stood for America, didn't she! She was living in England, but she was a bit of America. All right, she'd go down into the third form, she'd not even make a fuss. And if the girls teased her, she'd just show them she didn't care! But – she would try to get on with the work all right. Certainly she wouldn't slide down any further!

"You may go, Zerelda," said Miss Grayling, and Zerelda went. Miss Grayling watched her as she went gracefully out of the door. If only she could see herself as a proper little schoolgirl and not as Zerelda, the promising film star, how nice she might be!

On The Lacrosse Field

Miss Grayling sent for Miss Peters and told her that Zerelda was to come into her form.

"That will be hard for her," said Miss Peters. "Not the work, I mean – though I don't think Zerelda will find even third form work easy – but the disgrace."

"Sometimes hard things are good for us," said Miss Grayling, and Miss Peters nodded. After all, the girls didn't come to Malory Towers only to learn lessons in class – they came to learn other things too – to be just and fair, generous, brave, kind. Perhaps those things were even more important than the lessons!

"I don't know if you think it would be a good thing to say something to the third-formers before Zerelda appears in their classroom," said Miss Grayling. "You have one or two there – Gwendoline, for instance –

who might not be very kind. A word or two before-
hand might be as well."

"Yes. Just as well," said Miss Peters. "Well, I don't
expect an easy time for Zerelda, Miss Grayling. She's
got such funny ideas about things – spends all her time
on her appearance, you know – I've not much use for
that kind of girl."

"No," said Miss Grayling, thinking that probably it
would be good for Zerelda to have the hearty Miss
Peters over her for a little while. "Well – there's plenty
of good in the girl – she seems very good-humoured,
and I like her smile. Just say a few words to your form,
but don't make a big thing of it."

So, to the third form's intense surprise, Miss Peters
said the "few words" to them that afternoon in class.

"Oh, by the way," she said, "we are to have an
addition to our form. Zerelda Brass is coming to us."

Gwendoline drew in her breath sharply, and looked
round with a triumphant epxression. She was delighted to think that the American girl would now be
approachable – actually in her form, and in her
common room! Gwendoline could dance attendance
on her all she pleased. She would be her friend.

Miss Peters read Gwendoline's face wrongly.
"Gwendoline! I hope you will not delight in another
girl's inability to follow the work of a higher form. I
think . . ."

"Oh, Miss Peters!" said Gwendoline, a most hurt
expression on her face, "as if I would do anything of
the sort. I *like* Zerelda. I'm *glad* she'll be in our form. I
shall welcome her."

Miss Peters didn't know whether to believe this or
not. She disliked and distrusted Gwendoline. She
decided to give her the benefit of the doubt.

"It would be just as well not to discuss the matter with Zerelda if she would rather say nothing about it," she said. She cast a sharp look at Alicia. She knew Alicia's sarcastic tongue. Alicia looked back at her. She didn't mean to jeer at Zerelda – but at the back of her sharp-witted mind she knew that Zerelda's disgrace would be a nice little weapon to taunt her with, if she gave herself too high-and-mighty airs.

After the afternoon class there was half an hour's lacrosse practice. The third-formers streamed out, Gwendoline last as usual, with Mavis running her close. They were the despair of the games mistress. All the girls began to talk about Zerelda.

"Golly! Fancy being chucked out of a form like that!" said Irene. "Poor old Zerelda. I bet she feels awful."

"I should think she feels too ashamed for anything," said Mary-Lou. "I know how I should feel. I shouldn't want to look anyone in the face again!"

"I bet the fourth form are glad," said Jean. "Ellen told me they had got more order-marks because of Zerelda than they've ever had before! Let's hope she doesn't present *us* with too many. We haven't done too badly so far – except when Irene and Belinda leave their brains behind!"

"I think we all ought to be very nice to Zerelda," announced Gwendoline. "I think we ought to show her we're glad she'll be in our form."

Mavis looked at Gwendoline sourly. She knew quite well that once Zerelda appeared, she, Mavis, would lose Gwendoline's very fickle friendship. Nobody else had any time for Mavis. Gwendoline wasn't much of a friend, but at least she was somebody to talk with, and whisper to.

"Well," said Darrell. "Zerelda's got her faults, but she's jolly good-tempered and generous – and I vote we welcome her and show her we're glad to have her."

So, feeling rather virtuous and generous-hearted, the third-formers made up their minds to be very nice to Zerelda, and ease her disgrace as much as they could. They pictured her slinking into their form room the next day, red in the face, hanging her head, almost in tears. Poor Zerelda! She would be glad of their welcome.

"Darrell! Darrell Rivers! Come over here and I'll give you some catches," called the games mistress. Darrell ran up. She was a swift runner and loved lacrosse. How she longed to be in one of the match-teams. but it was hard for a third-former to be in a school team unless she was very big and strong.

"You catch well, Darrell!" called the games mistress. "One of these days you'll get into a match-team. We could do with a good runner and catcher in the third match-team."

Darrell glowed with pride. Oh! If only she *could* be in the match-team. How pleased her mother and father would be – and how she would boast to Felicity. "I was in the match-team when we went to play Barchester. I was on the wing because I'm so fast. And I shot a goal!"

She pictured it all as she ran to take another catch. Suppose she practised very hard indeed every minute she could? Should she ask Molly Ronaldson for extra coaching? Molly always said she was willing to give the juniors any tips if they were keen enough to come and ask for them.

But Molly was seventeen and Darrell was only fourteen. Molly seemed a very high-up, distant, rather grand person to Darrell, who hadn't really a very high opinion of herself.

She saw Molly as she was going off the field, hot and happy. She screwed up all her courage and went up to the big, sturdy girl shyly.

"Please, Molly – could I just ask you something? I do so want to be in one of the match-teams one day. Do you think there might be a *possible* chance if I do extra practice at catching – and – if you could give me any tips?"

As red as a beetroot Darrell stared at Molly, the famous games captain. Molly laughed and clapped Darrell on the back.

"Good kid!" she said. "I was only saying to Joan yesterday how you were coming on, and a spot of extra coaching would do you good. I'll send you the times I give extra practice to possible match-team players, and you can come along any of the times you're free."

"Oh, *thank* you, Molly," breathed Darrell, hardly able to speak for joy. "I'll come every time I can." She ran off, her face glowing. Molly had actually spoken to Joan about her! She had noticed her, and seen that she was coming on well. Darrell felt so happy that she leapt along like a deer, colliding with Mam'zelle round a corner, and almost knocking her over.

"Now, what is this behaviour?" said Mam'zelle, tottering on her high heels and clutching wildly at the wall. "Darrell! What are you thinking of, to come round the corner like a wild beast?"

"Oh, Mam'zelle – *sorry*!" cried Darrell, happily. "Honestly I didn't mean it. Oh, Mam'zelle, Molly Ronaldson is going to give me extra coaching at lacrosse. Think of it! I might be in the third match-team one day!"

Darrell ran straight into Mam'zelle

Mam'zelle was just going to remark that not for anything would she rejoice at that big Molly giving Darrell coaching at that extraordinary game lacrosse, when she saw Darrell's shining eyes. She had a soft spot for Darrell, and she smiled at her.

"I am very glad for you, *ma petite!*" she said. "It is indeed a high honour. But do not go round the corner and knock your poor Mam'zelle over in this way again. You have made my heart go patter-pit!"

"Pitter-pat, you mean, Mam'zelle," said Darrell, and ran off laughing.

She told the others what Molly had said. They were most impressed, all except those who disliked games. No one of the third form had ever been in a match-team, though one or two steady ones, such as Jean, had tried very hard. So had Sally.

"What with Bill rushing off to her horse every single minute, Irene rushing off to try out her new tune on the piano, Mavis trilling her voice, and now you, Darrell, racing off to practise catching from dawn to dusk, the third form will soon have a nice empty common room," said Alicia, a little jealous of Molly's notice of Darrell.

"Zerelda will be there to make up!" said Darrell. "I don't expect she'll mind our company there – she was always slipping into our common room till you stopped her, Jean."

Zerelda came to the third form classroom the next day, carrying her pencil box and paintbox, which she had forgotten to take to the form room the night before. She walked in looking quite unconcerned.

The third-formers immediately began to be nice. "Here, Zerelda – wouldn't you rather have this desk till Sally comes back?" said Darrell. "It's got a nice

65

position."

"No, Zerelda. You come and sit by me," said Gwendoline. "I should like that."

Alicia looked keenly at Zerelda. Zerelda looked exactly the same as ever! She didn't hang her head, she didn't look upset, she wasn't even red in the face.

"I don't believe she cares a bit!" thought Alicia. But Zerelda did. She cared terribly. It was very hard indeed to walk into the classroom of a lower form, knowing that everyone had been told that she had been sent down.

She wished they wouldn't try and be kind to her like this. It was nice of them, but she hated to think they were being nice because they were sorry for her.

"Keep your chin up, Zerelda!" she said to herself. "You're American. Fly the Stars and Stripes! Make out you don't mind a bit."

So, appearing quite unconcerned, she took the desk she had put her things in the night before, put in her pencil box and paintbox, and began to look for the book she would need for the first lesson.

The third-formers felt a little indignant. They had so virtuously and generously decided to welcome Zerelda, and help her not to mind what they considered to be a great disgrace – and *she* didn't seem to mind at all. She was exactly the same as usual, speaking in her slow drawl, fluffing up her hair, appearing even more sure of herself than ever.

Darrell felt rather annoyed. She considered that Zerelda ought to have shown a little more feeling. She didn't stop to think that Zerelda might be putting on a show of bravery, and that was all. Underneath it all the girl was miserable, ashamed and feeling very small.

Miss Peters came in briskly as usual. Mary-Lou

shut the door. Miss Peters swept keen eyes round the class. "Sit!" she said, and they sat. That keen glance had taken in Zerelda – but Miss Peters saw what the others did not see – a rather panic-stricken heart under all Zerelda's brave show. A hand that shook slightly as she picked up a book – a voice that wasn't quite so steady as usual.

"She feels it all right," thought Miss Peters. "But she's not going to show it. Well, she's got plenty of pluck. Let's hope she'll learn that she's not so important a person as she thinks she is. If we got right down to the real Zerelda, we might find somebody worth knowing! We *might*. I still don't know!"

The lesson began. Zerelda concentrated hard. She forgot her hair, her nails, her clothes. She really *worked* for about the first time in her life!

Bill and Miss Peters

Most of the third-formers were now almost settled in to their term's work. Alicia, however, was restless, missing Betty and not finding that Darrell quite made up for her old friend. Darrell was steady and loyal and natural – but she hadn't Betty's witty tongue, nor her daredevil ways. Still she was better than anyone else. Alicia hoped that Sally wouldn't be back till Betty came!

Bill was restless too. Bill got the idea that Thunder was pining for the other horses at home, and she was always disappearing to be with him.

"How you do coddle that horse!" said Alicia, in disgust. "I wonder he puts up with it."

Miss Peters was always pouncing on Bill for dreaming in class. Bill's standard of work was very uneven. She was brilliant at Latin, which she had taken continually with her brothers. She knew very little French, much to Mam'zelle's despair. She didn't know much maths because her brothers' tutor had devoted all his time to them at this subject and had not bothered much about her.

"He didn't think we did much maths in a girls' school," explained Bill. "But I do know my tables, Miss Peters."

"I should hope so!" groaned Miss Peters. "You will simply have to have extra coaching at maths, Wilhelmina."

"Oh, I can't," said Bill. "I spend every minute of free time with Thunder."

Miss Peters had known for some time now that Thunder was Bill's horse. She had seen him and admired him, much to Bill's delight. She had also marvelled at Bill's magnificent horsemanship. The girl rode as if she and her horse were one. She was never happier than when she was out riding with the others, galloping over the lovely country that lay behind Malory Towers.

But she was annoyed because she was only allowed to ride out with the others for company. She was not allowed to take Thunder out alone.

"But I do at home," she protested loudly. "I've gone off by myself for years and years and years. It's silly not to let me. What harm can I come to? I'm with Thunder all the time."

"Yes, I know all that," explained Miss Peters, patiently, for the twentieth time. "But you are not at home now, you are at school, and you have to do as the others do, and keep their rules. We can't have one rule for you and one rule for them."

"I don't see why not," said Bill, obstinately. She often sounded rude, because she was so much in earnest, and Miss Peters sometimes lost patience with her.

"Well, you are not running this school, fortunately," said Miss Peters. "You must do as you are told. And, Wilhelmina, if you insist on being silly about these things, I shall forbid you to see Thunder for two or three days."

Bill was dumbfounded. She stared at Miss Peters as if she couldn't believe her ears. She went red to the roots of her hair.

"But I couldn't not see Thunder," said Bill, trying to speak patiently. "You don't understand, Miss Peters. Though you *ought* to understand because you're so fond of horses yourself."

"I dare say," said Miss Peters, equally patiently. "But I'm not top-heavy about them, as you are – I mean, I don't think, dream, smell and ride horses every minute of the day and night as you do. Do be sensible, Wilhelmina. I'm putting up with quite a lot from you, you know, and it's time you pulled yourself together, and thought a little less of Thunder, and a little more of other things."

But that was just what Bill couldn't do, as the other third-formers soon found out. She wouldn't go for extra practice at lacrosse. She wouldn't go for a nature walk. She wouldn't even take on any of her extra duties in the common room, which everyone had to do

69

in turn. She got Mary-Lou to do them for her instead.

Mary-Lou was so gentle and kindly that she would do anything for anybody. Jean was very cross when she found Mary-Lou doing the flowers in the common room instead of Bill.

"Why are you doing this?" she demanded. "You can see on the list it's Bill's week."

"I know, Jean," said Mary-Lou, scared at Jean's sharp tone. "But Bill did so badly want to go and give Thunder an extra grooming today. He got so muddy yesterday."

"I'm getting tired of Bill racing off to the stables, never joining in anything the third form does, and getting other people to do her duties," said Jean. "I shall talk to her about it."

But she made no more impression on Bill than Miss Peters had done. Bill had spent her life with horses. She had, as Miss Peters said, thought, dreamt, smelt, groomed, and ridden horses all her life, and she just didn't want to do anything else.

She would have been excellent at lacrosse if she had practised. She was magnificent at gym, daring, supple and with a wonderful sense of balance. The gym mistress was delighted with her, and sang her praises to everyone.

Bill could turn cartwheels as easily as any clown in a circus, going over and over on hands and feet till the others were giddy with watching. She could fling herself in the air and turn a complete somersault. The gym mistress forbade anyone else to try and do it.

"You'll only damage yourselves," she said. But nobody else really wanted to turn somersaults in the air!

Bill could also walk on her hands, and the others

often made her perform to them in the evening when she could not go to the stables. Bill was good-natured and natural, and didn't get her head in the least turned by all the praise and acclamation given to her for her performances in gym or common room.

Zerelda watched and marvelled. She could not imagine how any girl could want to do such extraordinary things. She thought Bill was decidedly mad, but she couldn't help liking her. In fact, most of the girls liked her very much indeed, though they were annoyed and exasperated when she wouldn't join in with them over anything.

Belinda did some beautiful drawings of Thunder. She was very good at drawing animals, and when Bill saw them she exclaimed in delight.

"Belinda! They're simply marvellous! Please, please give them to me!"

"No," said Belinda, tucking them away into her portfolio. "I shall keep them with my collection of animal drawings."

"Well, Belinda, do some specially for *me*," begged Bill. "Oh, Belinda, you might. I'd have them all framed and stood on my dressing table."

"Gosh, Bill, you've got about six different photographs of horses there now," said Belinda. "You've no room for a picture of Thunder."

"I have! I should put him right at the very front," said Bill. "Belinda, *will* you do me some drawings of Thunder? I'll do anything for you if you will."

"Fibber!" said Belinda. "The only person you'll do anything for is Thunder. You wouldn't lift a finger to do anything for Miss Peters or for anyone in the third form and you know it."

Bill looked taken aback. "Am I really as bad as

that?" she asked, anxiously. "Is that what you all think of me?"

"Of course," said Belinda. "Why, you don't even take on your own duties. I heard Jean ticking you off for that – but Mary-Lou's going on doing them just the same. So you can't have a drawing of Thunder, my dear Bill, because if you do you'll only go and stand and gaze devotedly at him all the evening when you can't go to the stables, and that will make us crosser than ever."

Belinda paused to take breath. Bill looked as if she was going to fly into a temper. Then her sense of fairness came to help her.

"Yes. You're right, Belinda. I don't like you being right, but you are," she said, honestly. "I probably *should* keep flying upstairs to look at Thunder's picture if I had a really good one. And I'm sorry about making Mary-Lou do my duties after Jean told me about it. I'll tell her I'll do them all next week to make up."

"Right," said Belinda. "I'll draw you a fine picture of Thunder, with you on his back, if you like, if you keep your word. But – I shall jolly well take it away if you start being silly, because I'm only going to *lend* it to you till I see if you'll keep your promise."

Bill laughed. She liked Belinda. She liked Irene, too. They both did the maddest, silliest things, but they were fun, and you could always trust them to do the decent thing. She longed for a picture of Thunder – she only had a very bad photograph of him. Now she was going to get a lovely drawing!

Jean quite thought it was a belated result of her ticking-off that made Bill offer to do Mary-Lou's duties the next week. She was pleased.

72

Belinda kept her word and gave Bill a beautiful picture of Thunder, done in black charcoal, with Bill on her back in her riding breeches and a yellow jersey. Bill was absolutely thrilled. She made Mary-Lou walk into the village with her to try to get it framed at once. She couldn't buy a frame there, so she took one of the horse-photographs out of its frame on her dressing table and put Thunder's picture in it, neatly trimmed to fit.

Everyone admired it. "Now you remember, Bill, it's not yours *yet*," Belinda warned her. "It's only lent. The very next time you dodge out of duties or third form activities you'll find that picture gone!"

But although Bill was better from that day in trying to do some of the things her form thought she ought to do, she didn't get on very well with Miss Peters. She *would* sit and gaze out of the window, she *would* forget that her name was Wilhelmina, she would daydream and not pay any attention to either Mam'zelle or Miss Peters.

Mam'zelle complained bitterly. "This girl is not even polite! I say to her, 'Wilhelmina, do not dream' and she does not even bother to hear me and answer. I say to her, 'Wilhelmina, are you deaf?' and she still does not reply to me. Never, never will she learn any French – except for '*le cheval*'! Miss Peters, the only time I get that girl to turn round to face me is when I say suddenly the name of her horse. 'Thunder!' I say, and she turns round at once. She is mad that girl. All English girls are mad, but she is the most mad."

Miss Peters began to punish Bill in the way she resented and hated most. "Here is a returned maths lesson," she said to Bill. "Do it please, and until you have brought it to me again you must not go to see

73

Thunder was nuzzling into her hand for sugar

Thunder."

Or she would say, "Wilhelmina, you have paid no attention in class this morning. You will not go to the stables at all today."

Bill was angry and resentful – and disobedient! She was not going to stop seeing Thunder for anyone in the world. Least of all for Miss Peters! And so, to Jean's disgust, she ignored Miss Peters' punishments and slipped off to see Thunder whenever she liked.

Miss Peters did not even dream that Bill would disobey. "One of these days she'll find out, Bill," said Alicia. "Then you'll be for it! You really are an idiot."

What with Bill and her horse, Zerelda and her ways, Irene and Belinda with their feather-brains, and Mavis and her opera singing, Miss Peters considered that she had the most trying form in the school. "And all from North Tower too!" thought Miss Peters. "Really, I'm sorry for Miss Potts, their housemistress. They must drive her mad! Now I wonder when Wilhelmina is going to bring me that returned geography lesson. She won't go to see that horse of hers till she does!"

But Miss Peters was wrong. At that very minute Bill was in the stable and Thunder was nuzzling into her hand for sugar!

Alicia has a Parcel

The days flew by. It was still very cold and Gwendoline and Mavis complained bitterly, as they huddled

75

near the fire in the common room, or sat almost on top of the radiators.

"You should rush about a bit more in gym or on the lacrosse field," said Darrell, whose face was a rosy-pink with good health and happiness. She had gone out to the field every moment she could spare to have coaching from Molly. She was getting very good! She knew she was. Molly praised her catching and said it was excellent.

Gwendoline looked at Darrell with her usual scowl. She really felt miserable in the cold weather, for she came from an overheated home and could not get used to the fresh-air atmosphere of school. It annoyed her to see Darrell without a single chilblain, and to watch her race out happily into the frosty air for her lacrosse practice.

Belinda came slipping up behind Gwendoline, who was quite unaware that she was scowling. Belinda's quick pencil set to work. Mavis nudged Gwen.

"Look out! Here's Belinda again!"

Gwen turned round quickly, trying to smooth the scowl off her face – but it was difficult to feel angry and yet not scowl!

"Go away, Belinda! I don't want you to draw me!" she said peevishly. "I wish you'd leave me alone. I hate the way you come slinking up – I call it really sly."

"Oh no!" said Belinda. "I'm just interested in you, that's all. You have such a *lovely* scowl – the ugliest in the whole school, I should think. Do, do scowl again, Gwen, and let me draw it."

Gwen stopped herself from scowling, but it was a very great effort. Belinda grinned.

"Poor Gwendoline Mary – so annoyed, that it makes

her want to scowl more fiercely than ever – but she won't! Well, never mind – I'll watch for the next time."

She went away, and everyone laughed. Gwen's eyes filled with easy tears. She could always cry at any moment. How hateful Belinda was. Gwen thought she really must go and scowl at herself in the mirror, then she would see what was so unique about it. It probably was no worse a scowl than Mavis' or Bill's – but that horrid Belinda thought it was a fine way to tease her.

Darrell came in after her lacrosse practice, glowing and beaming. "I say, girls! What do you think? I may be a reserve for the third match-team! Only the third reserve – but it's something!"

"What's a reserve?" asked Zerelda, thinking it must be something marvellous, judging by Darrell's shining eyes.

"Well – if three girls fall out from the next match-team, I'd take the place of the third one," explained Darrell.

"Third reserves never play," remarked Alicia. "Everybody knows that. So don't hope too much, Darrell."

"I'm not," said Darrell. "Alicia, I do wish you would get a bit of coaching too. Molly's fine – takes no end of trouble."

"That fat, clumsy Molly!" murmured Zerelda, in her lazy drawl. "Gee – I just can't bear to look at her!"

It was silly of Zerelda to say things like that. It made Darrell and Jean and the rest of the keen lacrosse players annoyed. What did it matter what Molly looked like? She was a splendid games captain, and had won more matches than had been won for years by Malory Towers.

"She may be fat, but she's not clumsy – she's a fast runner and very powerful," said Darrell, stoutly.

"I'll say she is!" said Zerelda. "I met her running down the stairs the other day, and I thought there was an earthquake coming. But it was only her great feet pounding on the stairs. You can keep your Mollies! I don't want them. All brawn and no brains or charm!"

"And you, I suppose, are all charm, and no brains?" said Alicia's smooth, malicious voice. "How nice! Well, America can keep her Zereldas. They're not much good here!"

Zerelda flushed scarlet and bit her lip. The others held their breath, expecting an outburst. But it didn't come.

"I guess I asked for that," said Zerelda, stiffly, and she got up. She said no more, but went out of the room as gracefully as ever.

Nobody said anything. They felt uncomfortable. It wasn't right to taunt a girl when they had all decided to be nice to her – but on the other hand Zerelda was really very annoying and deserved to be ticked off.

"Where's Bill?" asked Darrell, to change the subject.

"Where do you suppose?" said Belinda. "Giving Thunder titbits in the stable."

"Well, I wish she wouldn't," said Jean. "It's absolutely flat disobedience, and she'll get into a terrific row if she's found out. I've argued with her and rowed her and told her to obey Miss Peters in case something worse happens – but she simply won't listen. I might as well talk to a stone wall."

"She says Thunder isn't well," said Mary-Lou.

"Imagination!" scoffed Alicia. "She just says that so that she can go and see him without *too* guilty a conscience."

"No. I am sure she really *does* think Thunder isn't well," said Mary-Lou, in her gentle voice. "She's very worried about him."

"Well, why doesn't she ask Miss Peters to get the vet to him?" said Irene.

"Because if she does Miss Peters will want to know how she knows he's not well," explained Mary-Lou. "And then the fat will be in the fire!"

"And there will be a sizzling noise and Miss Peters will go up in smoke!" said Belinda, taking out her pencil to draw Miss Peters going up in smoke.

Somebody put their head in at the common room door. "Hey there! Parcel post is in – and there's a parcel for you, Alicia."

"Thanks," said Alicia, and got up to go and get it. "Hope it's some chocolates from my godmother. She usually sends me a box each term."

She disappeared. Belinda finished her drawing and handed it round. Everyone yelled with laughter. Miss Peters was floating upwards, enveloped in smoke, and lightning was flashing from the smoke.

"Lovely!" said Darrell. "I wish I could draw like you. I can't do anything like that! You're lucky, Belinda."

"Yes, I am," said Belinda, taking back her drawing, and adding a few more strokes. "Don't know what I should do if I couldn't draw. I'd be miserable! Well, so would Irene be miserable if she couldn't have her music!"

"And I should be very very miserable without my voice," said Mavis at once.

"Yes. You'd be ten times more miserable than either Irene or Belinda," said Jean. "And I'll tell you

79

why. Because you just wouldn't be anything without your voice, Mavis! After all, Irene is good at maths, and she plays quite a good game of lacrosse, and she's always ready to have a bit of fun – like Belinda, who's pretty fair at everything besides being gifted at drawing. But you're nothing but a Voice! Take that away and I don't believe anyone would know you were here!"

"I can't help having a voice that overpowers the rest of me," said Mavis, complacently. "It's not my fault if I seem all Voice to you. When I'm an opera singer I shall . . ."

This was the signal for everyone to begin talking at the tops of their voices. It didn't matter what they said, they just talked to drown Mavis' familiar parrot-cry. As they talked they laughed to see her annoyed face, its small dark eyes gleaming spitefully.

Well – she didn't care! Wait till she was a bit older – then she would show the others what a gift like hers meant. She would sweep the whole world to rapture over her unique voice. Her family and her singing teachers marvelled at her voice, and were never tired of predicting a wonderful career. She could wait for that, even if it meant putting up with commonplace people like the third-formers!

Alicia came in with her parcel. "It's not from my godmother," she said, "so don't crowd around me too hopefully. It's from Sam."

Sam was one of her brothers, a scamp if ever there was one. The third-formers were never tired of hearing of his escapades.

"Is it some sort of joke to play, do you think?" asked Darrell, eagerly. "Alicia, you haven't played a trick for ages. I do hope it's a good one!"

80

Alicia opened the parcel. Out fell a small box. Belinda picked it up and looked at it. Something was written on the lid.

"Sneeze, Boys, Sneeze!"

"Whatever does it mean?" said Darrell, thrilled. "Let's open the box."

"Well, look out then," said Alicia, shaking out a letter from her brother. "Don't spill the contents. They may be valuable!"

Darrell opened the box. It was full of little white pellets, round and flat, about half an inch in diameter. "Whatever are they?" said Darrell. "And why the funny label on the box – 'Sneeze, Boys, Sneeze!' "

Alicia was reading Sam's letter and chuckling. "Listen to this," she said. "Sam really is a scamp. These pellets have been made by one of the boys in his form – he's a bit of an inventor in his way. What you do is to put a pellet on a shelf, damp it with a solution of salt water, and then leave it. In half an hour it sends off a kind of vapour that gets up people's noses and makes them sneeze terrifically!"

Everyone laughed. "Sam says he did it to his drawing master," said Alicia, chuckling again. "And he sneezed forty-three times. The boys counted. What a joke!"

"Let's play it on Miss Peters!" said Darrell, thrilled. "Oh, do let's!"

The idea of hearing the hearty Miss Peters sneezing forty-three times was very tempting. Alicia read Sam's letter to the end. "He says on no account must we use more than one pellet at a time, because the effects are very bad if too much vapour gets up anyone's nose. And he says the pellet-vapour only floats out about four feet – so if we do play the trick on Miss Peters, she will start sneezing her head off – but we shan't sneeze at all!"

"It sounds an absolutely super trick," said Darrell. "*Really* super! Alicia, we *must* play it. I should die of laughing to see Miss Peters sneezing like that. She has such a very terrifically loud sneeze – almost louder than anyone else's in the school."

"Well – we mustn't begin to giggle too soon or giggle too much in case Miss Peters smells a rat," said Alicia. "Though I don't see how she can. After all, *she* will be the only one who sneezes."

Everyone felt really thrilled. A trick on Miss Peters! Very few third-formers had ever dared to play jokes on her, for she was sharp, and so swift with punishment that usually nobody dared to annoy her too much. But this trick was surely foolproof!

"When can we play it? Tomorrow?" asked Darrell.

"No. Wait till we've got a test in maths or something," said Alicia. "Then, if Miss Peters sneezes too much we shan't have the test!"

The Days Go By

The next excitement was that Sally came back! Darrell was overjoyed. She hugged Sally, and they both began to talk at once.

"It's good to be back! I did hate not coming at the beginning of the term!"

"Oh, Sally, I have missed you! There's lots to tell you."

"You wrote awfully good letters. I'm longing to see Bill and Zerelda. Wasn't it a shame missing everything!"

Everyone was pleased to see Sally back – everyone that is, except Alicia. Alicia had got used to having Darrell for her companion and friend. Now she would have to share her with Sally – and she might not even be able to *share* her! Darrell might not want to bother with Alicia, with Sally back again.

So Alicia greeted Sally rather coolly, and made quite a show of being friendly with Darrell, hoping that Darrell would still want her for a friend. But Darrell forgot all about Alicia for a few days, she was so pleased that Sally was back.

There was so much news to exchange, so much to discuss. Sally marvelled at Zerelda and her ways, and heard two or three times all about how she had been taken from the fourth form and put into the third. She marvelled at Bill too and her prowess in the gym and on horseback. She thought Mavis and her voice were more difficult than ever to put up with. She was amused at the way Gwendoline followed Zerelda around and was not taken much notice of!

"Oh, Darrell – you don't *know* how good it is to be back again!" said Sally, happily. "I kept on and on thinking of you all – working in class – joking with Mam'zelle Dupont, and being ticked off by Mam'zelle Rougier – and playing lacrosse, and having fun in the gym, and roasting chestnuts by the fire in the common room. I was absolutely homesick for school!"

"Well, now you're back again at last," said Darrell. "I chummed up with Alicia whilst you were away, Sally. Betty's in quarantine for whooping cough and isn't back yet, so she was on her own and so was I."

Sally didn't very much like the idea of Darrell being friends with Alicia. She felt jealousy creeping up in her. Jealousy was one of Sally's failings. She had conquered it for some time – but it came slipping into her heart again now when she saw how friendly Alicia was with Darrell. She didn't like it at all.

So Sally was as cool with Alicia as Alicia was cool with Sally, and Darrell was surprised and grieved about it. She had hoped that once Sally had settled in, she and Sally and Alicia might be companions till Betty came back. It didn't seem to Darrell to be quite fair to throw off Alicia entirely, as soon as Sally came back.

Darrell told Sally about Alicia's proposed trick. Sally didn't seem to think it a good trick to play at all!

"It's silly to play a trick like that on Miss Peters," she said. "For one thing, she'll guess it's a trick and will deal out awful punishments – and for another thing I don't much like those tricks that make people have sneezing fits. I think they're a bit dangerous."

"Oh, Sally!" said Darrell, really disappointed. "I thought you'd be so thrilled. Don't be so prim and solemn! I believe it's just because it's *Alicia's* trick you don't like it!"

Sally was hurt. "All right – if you like to think things like that of me, you can," she said. "I suppose you think I'm jealous of Alicia. Well, I'm not. I can quite see why you like her so much – jolly, witty, amusing – all the things I'm not!"

Now it was Darrell's turn to look hurt. "You're silly, Sally," she said. "Yes, you are! You know you're my friend and I only went with Alicia and Alicia with me because you and Betty were away. Don't spoil things, Sally."

84

"All right. I'll try not to," said Sally, with an effort. But jealousy is a very hard thing to fight and an even harder thing to defeat. Try as she would Sally could not stop herself from being a little spiteful about Alicia, and she was so cool to her that Alicia, tickled to see her jealousy, began to play up to Darrell even more.

"Oh dear!" sighed Darrell to herself one afternoon as she ran out for a lacrosse practice, "why is it that Alicia is always so *specially* nice to me in front of Sally – and why has Sally changed so much? She *is* jealous, I know – but does jealousy change people such a lot?"

Darrell wasn't at all jealous herself. It was not in her nature, so she couldn't really understand Sally's feelings. She saw both sides very clearly. Sally didn't like Alicia and wanted Darrell's entire friendship. Alicia didn't see why she should give up Darrell's companionship completely just because Sally had come back. Why not a threesome till Betty returned?

"Well, I shan't think about *either* of them!" said Darrell, as she caught the lacrosse ball very deftly, spun round and sent it cleanly and swiftly to another player. So she didn't bother about anything except giving her whole attention to the fun of running and catching and throwing.

Molly Ronaldson was really pleased with her. It was not only Darrell's swiftness and deftness that made her pleased, but the girl's keenness. She had never missed a practice, she had come out in the coldest weather and the bitterest winds. She was a Good Sport – and Molly Ronaldson had no higher praise for anyone than that.

"Darrell Rivers, count yourself as third reserve for the third match-team," she said, as she went off the field with Darrell. "I'll put the notice up on the board this evening. There's always a chance you might play in a match, so keep up your practice. In this term there's such a lot of illness and people often fall out by the dozen."

"Oh, Molly – *thank* you!" said Darrell, finding it quite difficult to speak, she was so overcome. "I won't let you down – I'll not miss a single practice, even if it snows! I say, I do think it's super of you!"

"No, it isn't really," said Molly. "I'm thinking of the *team*. You're good enough – so in you go – as reserve first, with a faint chance of playing in a match later on."

Darrell rushed indoors, walking on air. Luckily she didn't collide with Mam'zelle round the corner this time. All she did was to bump into a bunch of fourth-formers, who scattered in alarm at her head-long rush.

"Darrell Rivers! Are you mad?" said Lucy.

"No! Well, perhaps I *am* a bit!" said Darrell. "I'm third reserve for the third match-team! Molly's just told me."

"That's jolly good," said Ellen. "Congratulations! Lucky thing! I'll never be in any match-team, and I'm a fourth-former."

Everyone seemed pleased and clapped Darrell on the back. She rushed to the third form common room to break the news there. Most of the girls were there, sitting about, reading, playing games or sewing. They looked up as Darrell burst in.

"Here comes the hurricane!" said Alicia, with a grin. "Shut the door, for goodness' sake, Darrell. There's an icy blast blowing round my legs already."

Darrell slammed the door. "Girls, I'm third re-serve!" she announced. "Molly's putting it up on the notice board tonight."

Alicia, who had been a little annoyed at Darrell's success at lacrosse that term, made up her mind to be pleased about it this time. It wouldn't do for her to be sour over this and Sally to be sweet! So she leapt up, thumped Darrell on the back, and yelled congratulations as if there had never before been anyone in the reserve.

She would hardly let Sally get near Darrell. Jean was pleased too, and Irene and Belinda came round to marvel. Even Mary-Lou added her bit, and Zerelda smiled and looked pleased, though secretly she wondered how anyone could possibly be so thrilled about such a peculiar thing. Altogether it was quite a triumph for Darrell, and she basked in the admiration with delight.

Sally was cross to see how pleased Alicia apparently was, and how Darrell welcomed her delight. "Oh dear!" she thought, "I am getting horrid! I can't even make myself say all the nice things to Darrell I'd like to say, just because Alicia got there first!"

Darrell was rather surprised that Sally didn't seem as pleased as she had expected her to be. "Aren't you glad, Sally?" she asked anxiously. "It's an honour for the third form, you know. Do say you're pleased!"

"Of course I'm pleased!" said Sally. "It's – it's fine. You've done jolly well, Darrell."

But she didn't sound very whole-hearted about it and Darrell felt faintly disappointed. Never mind! Alicia was thrilled – and so were the others. Perhaps Sally was still feeling a bit out of things, having come back so late in the term.

The next excitement was a notice put up on the board, next to the notice about Darrell, to say that

Miss Hibbert, the English mistress, was going to start rehearsals for "Romeo and Juliet". All third-formers were to go to the art room to be tried out for parts.

"Blow!" said Gwendoline, who didn't like Miss Hibbert because she had so often ticked her off for being affected and silly in her acting. "I was hoping she had forgotten about the play. It's such a waste of time."

"Oh *no*, it isn't," said Zerelda, who had brightened up very much at the notice. "Acting is marvellous! That's a thing I really *can* do. I did Lady Macbeth over in . . ."

"Yes, we know you did," interrupted Daphne. "We ought to know by now, anyway! You tell us often enough."

"I suppose you fancy yourself in one of the chief parts, Daphne?" said Alicia. "What a disappointment you'll get! Anyway, if Zerelda's so good, she'll play Juliet – if she can get rid of that American drawl!"

Zerelda looked alarmed. "Do you think my way of speaking will stop me having a good part?" she asked.

"Well – I can't imagine Shakespeare's Juliet talking with a pronounced American accent," said Alicia. "Still – if you act the part well enough I don't see why you shouldn't get it!"

Zerelda had been rather subdued lately, but now she came to life again, with the hope of starring in "Romeo and Juliet"! She paid a tremendous lot of attention to her appearance and spent as much time as she dared in front of her mirror. She also tried to get rid of her American drawl!

This amused the class very much. Zerelda had never made the slightest attempt before to speak in the English way and had laughed at the English accent and called it silly. Now she badgered everyone to tell her how to pronounce the words the way they did.

"Well, try to say 'won*d*erful' with the D in the middle, instead of 'wunnerful', for a start," said Darrell. "And say 'twen*t*y-four' with the T in the middle instead of 'twenny-four'. And couldn't you say 'stop' instead of 'starp' and 'shop' instead of 'sharp'? Or can't you hear the difference?"

Zerelda patiently tried to master the English way of speaking, much to Miss Peters' astonishment. She had felt quite pleased with Zerelda's efforts to keep up with the work of the form, but she was still annoyed with the girl's constant attention to her hair and appearance. Nor did she like Zerelda's still grown-up air, and her habit of appearing to look down on the others just because they were schoolgirls.

"Now I'll show them all!" thought Zerelda, studying the part of Juliet with great attention. "Now they'll see what I mean when I say I'm going to be one of the greatest of all film stars!"

Zerelda's Unfortunate Rehearsal

Miss Hibbert took a great deal of trouble in producing the school plays. She gave her time to each form in turn, and really achieved some excellent results. This term it was the third form's turn. They were to give the play towards the end of the term. They were thankful not to be doing French plays. Both the Mam'zelles took a hand in producing those, and as they had quite different ideas about acting, it was a little trying for the actors.

"Does Miss Hibbert choose the characters the first time?" asked Zerelda.

"Oh no – she tries us all out in almost every part several times," said Darrell. "She does that for two reasons – she says that in that way she really does find the right actor for every part – and we all get to know every part of the play and work better as a team."

"Gee, that's wunnerful – I mean, won*der*ful," said Zerelda. "I've been studying Juliet's part. It's a lovely one. Would you like to hear me do some of the lines?"

"Well – I'm just going to my lacrosse practice," said Darrell. "Sorry! Look – ask Alicia. She's got nothing to do this period."

But Alicia was not going to admire Zerelda's Juliet. She got up hastily. "Sorry! I've got to go to a meeting Zerelda. But I'm sure you'd be just wunnerful!"

"I'll hear you, Zerelda," said Gwendoline, glad of an opportunity to please the American girl. "Let's go into one of the empty music practice rooms, where you won't be disturbed. It will be lovely to see you act. I'm sure you must be awfully good. As good as – what's the star you like so much – oh yes, Lossie Laxton!"

"Well, maybe I'm not up to her standard yet," said Zerelda, fluffing up her hair in the way Lossie did on the films. "Okay, Gwen – we'll go to a practice room."

But they were all full, and music sounded from each of them, with the exception of one at the end. Irene was there, poring over a music score.

"I say, Irene," said Gwen, going in, "can you . . ."

"Go away," said Irene, fiercely. "I'm busy. Can't

you see?"

"Well, you're not needing the piano, are you?" said Zerelda. "Can't you do your work, whatever it is, somewhere else?"

"No, I can't. I shall want to try it out on the piano in a minute," said Irene. "Go away. Interrupting me like that!"

Zerelda was surprised. She had never seen Irene so annoyed before. But Gwendoline had. She knew that Irene could not bear to be disturbed when she was concentrating on her music, whether it was writing it out, or playing it on the piano.

"Come on," she said to Zerelda. "Let's go."

"Yes. GO!" said Irene, with a desperate expression on her face. "You've stopped me just when it was all coming beautifully. Blow you both!"

"Well, really, Irene, I do think you might let us use this room if you're only playing about with pencil and paper," began Zerelda. "I want to recite some lines of Juliet and . . ."

Then Irene went quite mad. She threw her music, her pencil and her music case at the alarmed Zerelda. "You're daft!" she shouted. "Give up my music-hour for your silly acting! Oh yes, I know you're going to be a wonderful film star, parading about in marvellous clothes, thinking of third-rate things if ever you *do* have a thought in your head – but what's all that compared to music! I tell you I'm . . ."

But Zerelda and Gwen did not wait to hear any more. They saw Irene looking round for something else to throw and as there was a vase of flowers on the little mantelpiece Gwen thought the sooner they went out of the room the better.

"*Well!*" said Zerelda. "If that doesn't beat all!

Irene's mad!"

"Not really," said Gwen. "It's only when she feels sort of inspired, and music comes welling up into her mind and she has to write it down. She's got the real artistic temperament, I suppose."

"Well, so have I," said Zerelda at once. "But I don't go mad like that. I wouldn't have believed it of her."

"She can't help it," said Gwendoline. "It's only when she's interrupted. Look – there's Lucy going out of one of the practice rooms. We can have that one if we're quick!"

They slipped into the room that Lucy had just left. Gwendoline sat down, ready to listen for hours if she could please Zerelda and make her feel really friendly towards her. Zerelda struck a lovesick attitude and began.

"Wilt thou be gone? It is not yet near day;
It was the nightingale and not the lark,
That pierced the fearful hollow of thine ear;
Nightly she sings on yon pomegranate tree;
Believe me, love, it was the nightingale."

Gwendoline listened with a rapt and admiring expression on her face. She had no idea at all whether Zerelda was good or not, but that made no difference to her praise.

"It's marvellous!" she said, when Zerelda at last stopped for breath. "However have you learnt such a lot? My goodness, you do act well. And you really look the part, Zerelda, with your hair and all."

"Do I?" said Zerelda, pleased. She always enjoyed herself when she was acting. "I know what I'll do. I'll shake my hair loose. And I'll wrap this tablecloth round me. No – it's not big enough. The curtain will do!"

To Gwendoline's amusement Zerelda took down the blue curtain and swathed it round herself over her brown school tunic. She undid her brilliant hair and shook it all over her shoulders. She decided to put the tablecloth round her too. Ah – now she felt more like Juliet. Holding her hands out pathetically in front of her she began another speech. It sounded really a little strange because Zerelda tried very hard to speak in the English way but kept lapsing into her usual drawl, so that the whole effect was rather funny.

Gwendoline wanted to laugh but she knew how offended Zerelda would be. The American girl paraded up and down, declaiming her speeches most dramatically, the blue curtain dragging behind her like a train, her hair almost hiding one eye.

Someone looked in. It was Bessie, a second-former. She had come to practise. But seeing two third-formers there, she fled. Then a fourth-former came. She was not scared of third-formers, but was very mush astonished to see Zerelda and her strange raiment.

"I've got to practise," she said, coming in. "Clear out."

Zerelda stopped indignantly. "Clear out yourself!" she said. "Gee, of all the nerve! Can't you see I'm rehearsing?"

"No, I can't," said the fourth-former. "And wait till a mistress sees you in that curtain – you'll be for it, Zerelda Brass. Clear out now, both of you. I'm late already."

Zerelda decided to go all temperamental like Irene. She caught up her book of Shakespeare's plays and threw it at the fourth-former. Most unfortunately at that moment Matron came by, and, as she always did, glanced into the practice rooms to see that each girl there was practising. She was filled with astonishment to see somebody wearing a curtain and a tablecloth, with hair all over her face, throwing a book at a girl about to sit down at the piano.

She opened the door sharply, making everyone jump. "What's all this? What are you doing? Oh, it's *you* Zerelda. What on earth have you got the curtain round you for? Are you quite mad? And what has happened to your hair? It looks a hundred times worse than usual. Janet, get on with your practising. Gwendoline, you shouldn't be here when a fourth-former is practising. As for you, Zerelda, if I see any more tempers like that, I shall report you to Miss Grayling! Throwing books at one another indeed! A third-former too! You'll go down into the first form if you behave like that!"

The girls couldn't get a word in, for Matron fired all this off at top speed. She pushed Janet firmly down on the stool, shooed Gwendoline out as if she was a hen, and took Zerelda firmly by the shoulder.

"You'll just come with me and let me find out if you've torn the cloth or the curtain," she said. "If you have you'll sit down in my room under my eye and mend it. And while I think of it – if you don't darn your stockings better than you have been doing, I shall have to ask you to come to me for darning lessons."

Angry and embarrassed, poor Zerelda had to walk down the corridor after Matron, trying to take the curtain and cloth away from her shoulders and waist, and wishing she could tie her hair back.

But Matron would give her no time to rearrange or

tidy herself. This stuck-up, affected American girl had annoyed Matron so often – now Matron was getting a bit of her own back! Let everyone see Zerelda in this rumpled, ridiculous state!

And most unfortunately for Zerelda they met a whole batch of giggling second-formers, who stared at Zerelda in delighted amazement.

"What's she done? Where's Matron taking her? Doesn't she look *awful*!" poor Zerelda heard the twelve-year-olds say. She blushed miserably and looked round for Gwen. But Gwen had gone. She knew Matron in this mood, and she wasn't going to go near her if she could help it!

They met Mam'zelle at the bend of the stairs, and Mam'zelle exclaimed in surprise. "*Tiens*! What is this? Zerelda! Your hair!"

"Yes. I'm dealing with her, Mam'zelle," said Matron, firmly. She and Mam'zelle were usually at war with one another, so Matron did not stop to talk, but swept Zerelda along to her room at top speed, leaving Mam'zelle to gape and wonder.

Fortunately for Zerelda, Matron could find no damage done to either the tablecloth or the curtain. She was quite disappointed! She did Zerelda's hair for her herself, and Zerelda was so overcome by Matron's briskness and ability to talk without stopping that she submitted without saying a word.

Matron plaited Zerelda's hair into two fat plaits! Zerelda had never had her hair plaited in her life. She sat there, horror-struck. This awful school! Whatever would happen to her next?

"There," said Matron, satisfied at last, tying the ends of the plaits with blue tape. She stepped back. "Now you look a proper schoolgirl, Zerelda – and very sensible and nice too. Why you want to go about pretending you are twenty, I don't know."

Zerelda got up weakly. She caught a glimpse of herself in the glass. How *awful*! Could that really be herself? Why, she looked a nobody – just like all the other English girls. She crept out of Matron's room and fled up to the dormy to try and put her hair right.

She met Miss Peters, who stared at her as if she didn't know her. Zerelda smiled a weak smile and tried to get by without a word.

"Well – *Zerelda*!" she heard Miss Peters say, as if she couldn't believe her eyes. Zerelda shot down the corridor, praying that she would not meet anyone else.

Gwendoline was in the dormy, and she too stared at Zerelda as if she was seeing a ghost.

"Did Matron do that to you?" she asked. "Oh, Zerelda – you look like a real schoolgirl now – not a bit like yourself. Oh, I *must* tell the others that Matron plaited your hair."

"If you dare to repeat such a thing I'll never speak to you again!" said Zerelda, in such a fierce voice that Gwen was quite scared. She shook her hair free of the plaits. "This horrible school! I'll never forgive Matron, never!"

Bill is Caught

Alicia had not been allowed to forget the sneezing trick. All the form begged her to do it – except Sally. Sally still said she thought it was a dangerous joke to play, but Alicia laughed at her.

"You only say that because it's *my* trick!" she said, knowing that Sally was jealous of her friendship with Darrell. "If it was Irene's joke or Jean's you'd be thrilled."

Jean was torn between her desire to see the trick played and her feeling that as head girl she ought not to be too encouraging. Still, head girls couldn't be too strict and prim – and she did badly want to see what would happen!

"There's to be a maths test next week," said Alicia. "That's the time to do it! I bet we'll get out of the test all right. A-tish-oo!"

Everyone laughed. Darrell hugged herself. Oh, school was such fun! She enjoyed every single minute of it. She loved her work and her play, she loved the company of the chattering girls, she loved being third reserve – oh, everything was wonderful! This was the nicest term she had ever had.

Then she saw Bill looking anything but happy. Poor Bill! She was worried because Thunder was still not himself. Nobody else seemed to notice it – but Bill *knew*. Thunder wasn't just homesick, as she had thought at first. He wasn't well. She was very worried about him – and the more worried she got, the less attention she paid to her work, and the crosser she made Miss Peters.

"Wilhelmina! Will you please pay attention! Wilhelmina! Will you repeat what I have just said? Wilhelmina, I will not have you in my class if you persist in looking out of the window and dreaming!" It was "Wilhelmina! Wilhelmina!" all the time.

It was dreadful. Bill was really very miserable now, but she said very little unless anyone actually asked her about Thunder. She knew that Jean disapproved strongly of her continual disobedience. But she simply couldn't help it! She must, *must* see Thunder each day, especially just now.

Miss Peters was beginning to be puzzled over Bill. If the girl was so fond of her horse, why did she keep earning punishments forbidding her to see him? Miss Peters thought back a few days. Why, Bill couldn't have seen her beloved horse all the week. And yet she hadn't complained about it!

A suspicion came into Miss Peters' mind. Was Bill being disobedient? Surely not! Disobedience was not a thing that Miss Peters had to deal with very often. Girls rarely dared to disobey even her slightest word. She was noted for her good discipline.

She spoke about it to Miss Potts, who was in charge of North Tower. "I'm puzzled about Wilhelmina, Miss Potts. I can't make her out. She is such a terrible dreamer, and yet she looks such a sensible, hard-headed little thing! Then, too, she seems so fond of that horse of hers – and yet although she knows I shall punish her by forbidding her to see him, she goes on being silly and getting punished! She can't have seen that horse of hers for a whole week now!"

Miss Potts looked startled. She frowned, trying to remember something clearly. "Well – that's funny – I could swear I saw Wilhelmina in the stables yesterday when I went by. I looked in at the windows as I passed – and I'm almost certain it was Wilhelmina – standing beside a big black horse."

"Yes – that would be Thunder," said Miss Peters, grimly. "The untrustworthy, disobedient little monkey! If I catch her disobeying I shall insist that the horse is sent back to her home. She can ride one of the school horses instead. I will not have her mooning all the morning over that horse, nice as he is – and being disobedient like that."

Miss Peters was really very angry. She never could bear to be disobeyed. She went back to her room, feeling shocked and disappointed. She hadn't thought Wilhelmina would be so deceitful and untrustworthy. It just showed her how little you knew about anyone!

Miss Peters felt more and more indignant about the whole thing as the day wore on. It so happened that she took the third form very little that day, as Miss Carton, the history mistress, Mam'zelle, Miss Linnie, the art mistress, and Mr Young, the singing master, each took the third form for a lesson. She had no chance of looking sharply at Bill to see if she looked guilty or not.

After dinner that morning there was about half an hour before afternoon school. This was a time when Bill very often slipped out to the stables. She usually went down the back stairs, out at a little side door, and across to the stables by a path under the trees, so that, unless she was very unlucky, nobody would see her.

She slipped off to the stables as usual to see

99

Thunder. He whinnied softly when he heard her footstep. She opened the big door and went inside. There was no one else there at all. Only the horses stamped and blew, glad of each other's company.

She went to Thunder's stall. He put his great black head into the crook of her arm and snuffled there happily. Bill stroked his velvety nose.

"Thunder, do you feel better? Let me look at your eyes. Oh, Thunder, they aren't as bright as they ought to be – and I don't like the feel of your coat. It should be much silkier. It's harsh. Thunder, what's wrong? Don't be ill, darling Thunder, I couldn't bear it."

Thunder blew a little and whinnied happily. He didn't feel well, certainly – but that didn't matter when Bill was with him. He could feel ill and yet be happy at the same time if she was with him.

Upstairs in North Tower, Miss Peters walked along the corridor. She meant to find Bill and have a straight talk with her. She went to the door of the third form common room and looked in. Wilhelmina was not there!

"I want Wilhelmina," said Miss Peters. "Where is she?"

Everybody knew, of course. But nobody was going to tell. Darrell wondered if she could possibly slip out and warn Bill to come back quickly.

"Shall I go and find her for you?" she said.

"No. I'll find her," said Miss Peters. "Does anyone know where she is?"

Nobody answered. They all looked blank in a most irritating way. Miss Peters felt furious. She knew quite well that they all knew. Well, she couldn't expect them to sneak, if they thought Wilhelmina was some-where she ought not to be – in the stables!

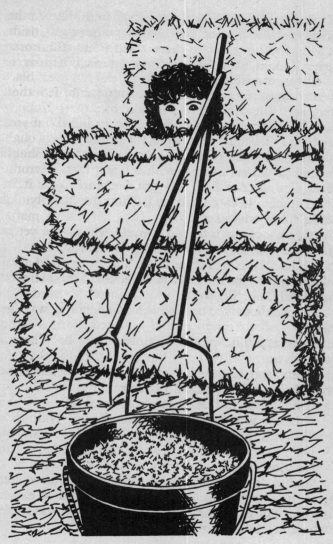

Darrell and Bill tried to hide

"I suppose she is in the stables," said Miss Peters, grimly. She looked at Jean. "You, as head girl, Jean, ought to tell her not to be so foolish and dishonourable. You know I put everyone on their honour to obey any punishment I give."

Jean went red and looked uncomfortable. It was all very well for Miss Peters to talk like that! Nobody could possibly make any impression on Bill if it meant that she would have to neglect Thunder!

"Stay here, all of you," commanded Miss Peters, feeling sure that one or the other might rush off to the stables to warn Bill if they got a chance. And Miss Peters meant to catch Bill herself and stop this kind of thing for good and all.

"Oh, poor Bill!" groaned Darrell, when Miss Peters had gone. "Now she'll get into a fearful row! I say – I bet Miss Peters has gone down the front stairs. If I race down the back ones, I *might* get to the stables first and warn Bill. I'll try!"

She didn't wait to hear what anyone had to say. She shot out of the room, almost knocked down Matron outside, raced down the corridor to the back stairs, went down them two at a time, slid through the side door and out under the trees. She shot over to the stable door and squeezed through it.

"Bill! Look out! Miss Peters is coming here!" she hissed. She saw Bill's startled face beside Thunder's black head.

Then she heard footsteps and groaned. "It's too late – you'll be caught. Can't you hide?"

Darrell shot under a pile of straw and lay there, her heart beating wildly. Bill stood as if turned to stone, her freckled face pale with fright. The door opened wide and Miss Peters came in.

"Oh! So you *are* here, Wilhelmina!" she said, angrily. "I suppose you have been systematically disobeying me the whole week. I am really ashamed of you. You will never settle down at school whilst you have Thunder here, I can quite see that. He will have to be sent back home in a horsebox."

"No! Oh no, Miss Peters! Don't, don't do that!" begged Bill, even her freckles going pale with anxiety. "It's only that Thunder's not well. He really isn't. If he was well I'd obey you. But he needs me when he's not well."

"I'm not going to discuss the matter," said Miss Peters, coldly. "You have heard what I said. I am not likely to change my mind after such a show of disobedience. Please go back to your common room, Wilhelmina. I will tell you when I have made arrangements to send Thunder home and you can say goodbye to him till the holidays. It will probably be the day after tomorrow."

Bill stood still, quite petrified. She couldn't make her legs move. Darrell couldn't see her, but she could imagine her very well indeed. Poor, poor Bill.

"Go, Wilhelmina," said Miss Peters. "At once please."

And Bill went, her feet dragging. Darrell heard a smothered sob. Oh dear – what a pity she had to hide under this straw and couldn't go and comfort Bill. Never mind – Miss Peters would soon be going, and then Darrell could fly up to the common room and sympathize warmly and heartily with Bill.

But Miss Peters didn't go. She waited till Bill had quite gone. Then she went over to Thunder and spoke to him in such a gentle voice that Darrell could hardly believe it was Miss Peters'! "Well, old boy," said Miss

Peters, and Darrell heard the sound of her hand rubbing his coat. "What's the matter with you? Don't feel well? Shall we get the vet to you? What's the matter with you, Thunder? Beautiful horse, aren't you? Best in the stables. What's up, old boy?"

Darrell could hardly believe her ears. She wriggled a little in the straw so that she could get a hole to peep through. Yes, there was Miss Peters, standing close to Thunder, and he was nuzzling her and whinnying in delight. Why, Miss Peters must love him! Of course, she was very fond of horses, Darrell knew that. But this was different somehow. She really seemed to love Thunder as if he was her own horse.

Miss Peters gave thunder some sugar and he crunched it up. Then she went out of the stable and shut the door. Darrell got out of the straw and shook herself. She went to the door and listened. Miss Peters had gone. Good!

She opened the door and went out – and then she stood still, thunderstruck. Miss Peters *hadn't* gone! She was just outside, doing up her shoelace! She looked up and saw Darrell coming out of the stables.

She stood up, red with rage. "What were you doing in there?" she demanded. "Were you there all the time I was talking to Wilhelmina? You were in the common room when I left. Did you actually dare to run down the back stairs to warn Wilhelmina?"

Darrell couldn't speak. She nodded. "I shall deal with you later," said Miss Peters, hardly trusting herself to speak. "What the third form is coming to I really do not know!"

Bill would not be comforted by Darrell or anyone else. She hadn't gone to the common room as Miss Peters had told her to. She had gone to the dormy and wept by herself. Bill boasted that she never cried, but this time she did. Her seven brothers had taught her to be tough and boyish, and, like a boy, she had scorned ever to shed a tear.

But she couldn't help it now. When she appeared for afternoon school the third-formers saw her red eyes and came round her to comfort her. But she pushed them away. Darrell was pushed away too, though Bill spoke a few words to her, very gratefully.

"Thank you for coming to warn me. It was decent of you, Darrell."

"Bill – it's a shame," began Darrell. But Bill turned away.

"I can't talk about it," she said. "Please don't."

So the third-formers gave it up, and looked at one another helplessly. You simply couldn't do anything with Bill if she didn't want you to. Darrell took her place in class that afternoon with much trepidation. She knew she would sooner or later be called to Miss Peters' room, and she wondered what would happen to her. Oh dear – and everything had been so lovely up till then. Now she had got herself into trouble, and she had only wanted to help poor Bill.

Miss Peters was in a grim mood that afternoon. She was looking out for anyone or anything that would feed her anger. But nobody, not even Mavis, Gwendoline or Zerelda, did anything to provoke her. Miss Peters was terrifying when she was like this. Her big, heavy face was red, her eyes flashed as they looked round the class, and her short hair seemed to cling more tightly to her head than usual!

All the third-formers felt miserable that evening, with Bill sitting like a figure of stone in a corner. It was Mavis who suddenly livened them up.

"I say," she said, in a whisper, as if somebody was listening who shouldn't be there. "I say! Look here!"

She held up a paper. On it were printed these words:

TALENT SPOTTING!

Have you a gift? Can you play the piano well? Can you draw? Do you sing?

Then bring your talent to the Grand Hall, Billington, on Saturday night, and let us SPOT your TALENT.

Big prizes – and a CHANCE to make your NAME!
TALENT SPOTTING!

The girls read it. "Well, what about it?" said Alicia. "Surely you are not thinking of being spotted for talent, Mavis?"

"Yes, but listen," said Mavis, still in an urgent whisper, "what about Irene going with her music – and Belinda with her drawing – and Zerelda with her acting – and me with my voice? Think what prizes we would win!"

Everyone stared at Mavis scornfully. "Mavis! As if

we'd *ever* be allowed to go!" said Belinda. "And besides, who wants to go to a fifth-rate affair like this? Talent spotting indeed! Just a silly show put on to amuse the people of Billington! And the prizes will probably be half-crowns! Don't be so silly."

"But, Belinda – Zerelda – it's such a chance!" said Mavis, who had imagined herself standing on the platform and filling the hall with her lovely voice, being applauded to the echo and perhaps having her name in the papers. Poor, foolish Mavis. Her conceit blinded her to what the show really was – just a village affair got up for fun.

"Mavis, you're just too silly for words," said Alicia, impatiently. "Can you honestly see Miss Grayling allowing Malory Towers girls to go to a thing like this and make themselves cheap and idiotic? Do use your common sense."

"She can't. She hasn't got any," said Daphne.

Mavis snatched the paper from Darrell, who was reading down it with a grin. "All right," she said. "If you don't want a bit of fun, you needn't have it. I've a good mind to go on my own."

"Don't be a fathead," said Jean. "Think of yourself standing up on a big platform, just a schoolgirl, singing to a crowded hall. It's ridiculous!"

But it didn't seem a ridiculous picture to Mavis. She could see it all very clearly. She could even hear the thunderous applause. She could see herself bowing time after time. It would be a little taste of what life would be like when she was an opera singer!

She stuffed the notice into her pocket, wishing she hadn't said anything about it. But a little thought kept slipping into her mind, exciting her, making her restless.

"Suppose I go? Nobody would miss me if I said I was going for an extra lesson in singing. They would just think Mr Young was making up the lesson he missed last week."

It was a very exciting thought. Today was Thursday. Mavis decided to think about it all Friday and make up her mind on Saturday. Yes, that was what she would do – then she could make her plans in good time if she decided to go!

She thought about it all day Friday. And Bill thought about Thunder. Neither of them dared to be too dreamy in class, but fortunately Miss Peters did not take the third-formers a great deal that day, having to take duty for another teacher who was ill. Mam'zelle came to take her place, and she was in a pleasant mood, very talkative, and not very observant. So Bill and Mavis were able to do a little dreaming in peace.

Bill had not dared to go to the stables again. She was hoping against hope that Miss Peters might change her mind and relent. Perhaps she would let Thunder stay after all. So she did not go near the stables, hoping that Miss Peters would tell her she was not going to be so harsh after all.

Miss Peters still had not said anything to Darrell. The girl wished she would get it over, scold her, punish her – but not keep it hanging over her like this. Perhaps that was part of Miss Peters' plan though to keep Darrell on tenterhooks for a few days!

Saturday came. Mavis had made up her mind. She would go! She would tell Miss Potts she had a singing lesson. She often had extra singing at odd times, so Miss Potts would not think it at all strange. She would tell the girls that too. She wouldn't be back early enough for nine o'clock bedtime but she trusted the girls not to give her away. She would slip in up the back stairs.

So Mavis made her plans. She looked up the buses. She meant to catch the six o'clock bus. That would get her to Billington at seven. The show began at half-past. She could easily go into the hall and find out what she had to do.

She looked up the buses back. How long would the show last? About two hours, probably. There was a bus back at half-past nine – the last one. Goodness, it was late!

Mavis began to have a few qualms about her adventure. It was very, very late for her to come back alone in the dark all the way up the school drive from the bus stop. Oh dear – would it be moonlight? She did hope so!

Bill came over to Darrell on Saturday morning. "Darrell! Would you do something for me? I'm not going to go to the stables again unless I'm allowed to – just in case Miss Peters might change her mind about sending Thunder away – so would you *please*, Darrell, slip down there yourself and go to Thunder and see if he's all right?"

"Yes, of course," said Darrell. "He wasn't out with the other horses this morning. I saw them all go off, but Thunder wasn't there."

"No, he wouldn't be," said Bill. "Nobody rides him but me. Do go, Darrell."

Darrell went. It didn't matter *her* going in the least. She kicked herself for not having thought of it before. She could have gone yesterday for Bill too.

She went into the stables. All the horses were there. One of the grooms was there too, rubbing a horse down, whistling between his teeth as he did so.

"Morning, Miss," he said.

"Good morning," said Darrell. "Where's Thunder? Is he all right?"

"He's over there in his stall, Miss," said the groom, standing up. "He doesn't seem too well. It's my opinion he's in for a bout of colic or something."

Colic? That was tummy-ache, wasn't it, thought Darrell. Oh well, that wasn't anything very much. She went over to Thunder, who hung his head and looked miserable.

"He really doesn't seem very well, does he?" said Darrell, anxiously. "Do you suppose he's missing his mistress? She's not been allowed to see him."

"Well, he may be," said the groom. "But it's his insides are making him miserable, I guess. Have to have the vet to him if he doesn't pick up. But I did hear something about him being sent back home."

Darrell said no more. She ran back to North Tower to find Bill, who was anxiously waiting for her.

"Thunder doesn't seem *very* well," she said. "But you needn't worry. The groom said it was only that he might be going to have a bout of colic. That's nothing, is it?"

Bill stared at her in horror. "Colic! Why, it's one of the worst things a horse can have! Oh, Darrell, think what a big stomach a horse has and imagine him having an ache all over it. It's *agony*!"

"Oh – I didn't know," said Darrell. "But – surely it isn't as serious as that, is it?"

"It is, it is," said Bill, and tears came into her eyes. "Oh, what shall I do? I *daren't* go to the stables in case I'm caught, and I might spoil Thunder's chance of not being sent home after all. Miss Peters hasn't said anything more to me about him going. Oh, what *shall*

I do?"

"You can't do anything," said Darrell. "Really you can't. He'll be all right tomorrow. Don't you worry, Bill. Oh, blow – it's begun to pour with rain – just as I wanted to go and practise catching again."

Bill turned away. Rain! What did *rain* matter! She sat down in a corner and began to worry hard. Colic! One of her brothers' horses had had colic and had died. Suppose – suppose Thunder got very ill in the middle of the night – and nobody knew? The grooms did not sleep very near the stables. *Nobody* would know. And in the morning Thunder would be dead!

Whilst Bill tortured herself with these horrible thoughts, Mavis delighted herself with pleasant ones. She had made all her plans. She didn't care a bit if she was discovered after it was all over – by that time she could have been received with wonder and applause, and Malory Towers would praise her and admire her.

"How bold she is to do a thing like that!" they would say. "Just the kind of thing an opera singer *would* do! All fire and temperament and boldness! Wonderful Mavis!"

Nobody had any suspicion of Mavis' mad plans that night. Miss Potts said nothing when she told her that she was to have an extra singing lesson, and would be having her supper early to make time for it. The girls took no notice either. They were used to Mavis and her odd lessons at all times.

"It's all too easy for words!" thought Mavis, ex-ultantly. "I shall easily be able to catch the bus. Nobody will guess a thing! Whatever will the girls say when I come back tonight! Well – they'll know I am something besides just a Voice!"

She caught the bus easily. It was pouring with rain,

but she had her mackintosh with her. She did not wear a hat in case somebody noticed the school-band, so her head was bare. But as the bus stopped just by the Grand Hall at Billington, she wouldn't get her hair very wet.

The bus started off with a jolt. Off to fame! Off to applause! Off to the Beginning of a Wonderful Career!

Where is Mavis?

Miss Potts noticed that Mavis was not at the supper-table. She was about to remark on it when she remembered that Mavis had told her something about an extra singing lesson. She must have had supper early then, as she sometimes did when Mr Young came late. So Miss Potts said nothing.

The girls thought nothing of it either. They were used to Mavis and her continual extra voice-training now. They hardly missed her. As they often said, Mavis was really nothing but a Voice and a lot of conceit.

Bill was very silent and worried, and ate hardly anything. Warm-hearted Darrell felt sorry for her. She knew she was worrying about Thunder and not being able to go to him. She whispered to Bill.

"Shall I go and have a look at him for you after supper?"

Bill shook her head. "No. I don't want to get you into trouble. Nobody's allowed in the stables when it's dark."

112

No one said anything about Mavis not being in the common room after supper. Alicia switched on the wireless. Belinda began to do a ridiculous dance. Zerelda got up and joined her. Everyone laughed. Zerelda could be really funny when she forgot her airs and graces.

She was pleased at the girls' applause. "Shall I act a bit of 'Romeo and Juliet' for you?" she asked, eagerly. "I'm tired of waiting for that rehearsal with Miss Hibbert!"

"Yes, do, Zerelda!" said Gwen, at once. The others were not too keen, but they sat back, prepared to be patient for a little while.

Zerelda began. She struck a pose, lifted up her voice and began to speak and act the part of Juliet, trying to talk in the English way.

The result was so very comical that the girls roared with laughter. They honestly thought that Zerelda was being funny on purpose. Zerelda stopped and looked at them, offended.

"What are you laughing at? This part is very tragic and sad."

Still the girls thought that Zerelda was being funny, and they laughed again. "Go on, Zerelda! This is priceless!" said Darrell. "I never knew you could be so comical."

"I'm not being comical," said Zerelda.

"Do go on," begged Irene. "Come on – I'll be Romeo. We'll rag the whole thing."

"I'm *not* ragging," said Zerelda. "I was playing the part properly – as I thought it ought to be played."

The girls looked at her in surprise. Did she really mean it? Did she honestly think that kind of acting was good? It was so bad that it was funny.

They didn't know what to say. They could, however, quite well imagine what Miss Hibbert would say. She had her own way of dealing with stage-struck people who thought they could act. Zerelda was appalling. She flung her hands about, made terrible faces which were supposed to be tragic, and was altogether too dramatic for words.

"She can't act for toffee!" whispered Alicia to Darrell. "What are we to say?"

Fortunately the door was opened at that moment and a fourth-former came in to borrow a gramophone record. Zerelda, offended with everyone, sat down in a chair and took up a book. She hated everyone in the school! Why had she ever come here? Not one of them thought anything of her – and she was worth the whole lot put together.

When the bell rang at nine o'clock Mavis was not back. Jean noticed it at once. "Where's Mavis? I haven't seen her all evening."

"She said she had a singing lesson," said Darrell. "But what a long one it must have been! Well, she'll come along when Mr Young's finished with her, I suppose."

"He's never as late as this," said Jean, puzzled. "I wonder if I ought to tell Miss Potts."

"No, don't. She may be messing about somewhere, and you'll only get her into trouble," said Belinda. "She'll be up in the dormy probably."

But she wasn't. The girls undressed and got into bed. Jean did not allow talking after lights out, so there was nothing said until Jean herself spoke.

"I say! You don't think, do you, that that idiot of a Mavis has gone off to that talent spotting affair? You know – the thing at Billington Grand Hall."

114

There was silence. Then Alicia spoke. "I shouldn't be a bit surprised! She's quite silly over her voice. She might think it was a wonderful chance to air it in public. She's always wanting to."

"Well!" said Jean, angrily, "she'll just *have* to be reported then. Honestly, she's the limit."

"We can't do much just now," said Darrell. "She may be back at any minute. I forget what time the concert began. I expect she'd catch the half-past eight bus back and be here just after half-past nine. It must be nearly that now. You'll have to report her tomorrow morning, Jean – what a perfect idiot she must be, if she really *has* gone!"

"What I'm afraid of," said Jean, "is that they might let her get up on the platform and sing – and, you know, she really had got such a wonderful voice that it would be bound to bring the house down – and that's just what Mavis would love – cheering and clapping and applause! She'll be worse than ever if that happens – and she won't care a bit about being reported and punished."

"Leave it till tomorrow morning," said Darrell, sleepily. "She'll be along soon. Tick her off then, Jean, and report her in the morning."

Miss Potts heard the voices in the dormy and was surprised. She came to the door – but as she heard Jean's clear voice say "Now, no more talking, girls" at that moment, she did not open the door to scold. If she had, she would have switched on the light and noticed Mavis' empty bed. As it was, she went away at once.

The girls were tired. Jean tried to keep awake to tick off Mavis, but she couldn't. Her eyes closed and she fell fast asleep. So did everyone else – except Bill. Bill hadn't heard a word about Mavis. She was wrapped up

115

in her own thoughts and they were very miserable ones. Thunder! How are you getting on? Have you missed me? Bill talked to Thunder in her thoughts, and heard nothing else at all.

Darrell too was asleep. She had meant to have a last comforting whisper with Bill, who slept next to her, but she fell asleep before she could say the words. Only Bill was awake.

Mavis didn't come. Ten o'clock struck, and eleven. No Mavis. All the girls were asleep except Bill, and she didn't think about Mavis. Twelve o'clock struck. Bill counted the strokes.

"I can't go to sleep! I simply can't! I shall lie awake till the morning. If only I knew how Thunder is getting on! If I knew he was all right, I'd be all right, too. But supposing he really has the colic?"

She lay and thought for a few minutes. She remembered a window that overlooked the stables. If she went to it and opened it and leaned out, she might perhaps hear if Thunder was all right. A horse with colic makes a noise. She would hear that.

Bill got out of bed, and felt for her dressing gown and slippers. She put them on. She groped her way to the door, bumping against Darrell's bed as she did so. Darrell woke up at once.

She thought it was Mavis coming back. She sat up and whispered loudly. "Mavis!"

No answer. The door softly opened and shut. Somebody had gone out, not come in. Who was it?

Darrell got her torch and switched it on. The first thing she saw was Bill's empty bed. Was Bill ill? Or had she gone to the stables? Surely not, in the middle of a pouring wet night!

She went to the door and opened it. She thought she

saw something a good distance down the corridor. She ran after the something.

Bill had gone to the window that overlooked the stables. She opened it, and Darrell heard her and went towards the sound. Bill leaned out of the window and listened.

Her heart went cold! From the stables came a groaning and a stamping. There was a horse in distress there, quite certain. Bill knew it was Thunder. She felt sure it was. He had colic! He was in agony. He would die if somebody didn't help him!

She turned away from the window and jumped violently when Darrell put a hand on her shoulder. "Bill! What are you doing?" whispered Darrell.

"Oh, Darrell – I was listening to see if any noise came from the stables over there – and there's a horse in pain. I'm sure it's Thunder. I must go to him! Oh, Darrell, please come with me. I might want help. Do, do help me."

"All right," said Darrell, unhappy to hear Bill's tearful voice. "I'll come. Come back and get on something warmer. It's pouring with rain. We can't go out in dressing gowns."

Bill didn't want to stop to put anything on, but Darrell made her. The two girls put on cardigans and tunics and mackintoshes. Then they slipped down the back stairs, went through the little side door and ran across to the stables in the pouring rain.

Darrell could hear a horse groaning and stamping. Oh dear! It sounded awful. With trembling fingers Bill undid the stable door and went inside. There was a lantern standing in a corner, with a box of matches beside it. Her fingers trembled so much that she couldn't strike a match and Darrell had to light the lamp.

Both girls felt better when the light streamed out into the dark stable, that smelt of horses and hay. Bill made her way swiftly to Thunder's stall. Darrell followed with the lantern.

Thunder's eyes were big and frightened. He hung his head in misery. From his body came weird rumbling noises, like far-away thunder.

"Yes. He's got colic. He's bad. Darrell, oh, Darrell, we mustn't let him lie down. That would be fatal. We must walk him about all the time."

"Walk him about? Where?" asked Darrell, in astonishment. "In the stables?"

"No. Outside. It's the only thing to do, keep him walking so that he can't lie down. Look, he's trying to lie down now. Help me to stop him!"

But it is a very difficult thing to prevent a big horse from lying down if he wants to! Neither of the girls would have been able to stop him if Thunder had really made up his mind to lie down – but fortunately he decided to stand up a little longer and nuzzle against Bill. He was so very, very glad to see her!

Bill was crying bitterly. "Oh, Thunder! What can I do for you? Don't lie down, Thunder. Don't lie down!"

"You ought to have the vet, Bill, oughtn't you?" said Darrell, anxiously. "How can we get him?"

"Could you possibly ride over and fetch him?" said Bill, wiping her eyes with the back of her hand. "You know where he lives – not far off, really."

"No, I couldn't," said Darrell. "I don't ride well enough to get a horse and gallop off on a dark night. You go, Bill, and I'll stay with Thunder."

"I can't leave him even for a *minute*!" said Bill. She

118

seemed quite unable to think what to do. Darrell thought hard.

An idea came into her head. She touched Bill on the shoulder. "Bill! Stay here and I'll get help somehow. Don't worry. I'll be back as soon as I can!"

A Midnight Ride

Darrell raced off into the rain. She had thought of something – but she didn't want to tell Bill what it was. Bill wouldn't like it. But still, it was the only sensible thing Darrell could think of.

She was going to wake up Miss Peters and tell her about Thunder! She remembered how she had heard Miss Peters talking to the horse, sympathizing with him, and she remembered, too, how Thunder had nuzzled happily against her. Surely Miss Peters would understand and come to their help?

She went indoors. She made her way to Miss Peters' room, stumbling through the dark corridors. She wondered if she had come to the right room. Yes, this must be it. She rapped at the door.

There was no answer. She rapped again. Still no answer. Miss Peters must sleep very, very soundly! In desperation Darrell opened the door and looked in. The room was in darkness. She felt for the light switch and put it on.

Miss Peters was lying humped up in bed, fast asleep. She slept very soundly indeed, and even a thunderstorm did not usually awaken her. Darrell went to the bed and put her hand on Miss Peters' shoulder.

Miss Peters awoke at once then. She sat up and stared at Darrell in amazement. "What is it?" she said. "What have you come to me for?"

Darrell would have gone to Miss Potts or Matron in the usual way – but this was something so unusual that the girl felt only Miss Peters could deal with it properly. She began to tell Miss Peters all about the trouble.

"It's Thunder. He's got colic and Bill's afraid he'll die if he lies down. Can you get the vet, Miss Peters?"

"Good gracious! Have you and Bill been out to the stables at this time of night?" said Miss Peters, looking at her clock, which showed half-past twelve. She sprang out of bed. She pulled on riding-breeches and jersey and riding-coat, for she had been riding that day with the school, and her things lay ready to hand.

"Yes," said Darrell. "But don't be angry, Miss Peters – we simply had to go when we heard Thunder in pain."

"I'm not angry," said Miss Peters. "I was worried myself about Thunder today. I rang up the vet and he said he would come tomorrow. I'll come down with you and have a look at the horse myself."

In a few minutes she was in the stables with Darrell. Bill was amazed to see her, but very comforted when she saw how capably Miss Peters handled the distressed horse. Thunder whinnied to her and nuzzled against her shoulder. Miss Peters spoke to him gently, and Bill's heart warmed to her.

"Oh, Miss Peters – can we get the vet to come now? I'm so afraid Thunder will lie down and we won't be able to get him up again."

Thunder's insides gave a most alarming rumble just then and he groaned in pain and fright. He seemed about to lie down, but Miss Peters took him out of his stall at once, and began to walk him up and down the stables. The other horses looked round, mildly surprised at all these unusual happenings. One or two whinnied to Miss Peters. They were very fond of her.

"Darrell! Go quickly and get sou'westers for yourself and Bill. Then take the horse into the yard and walk him round and round. I'll go and phone the vet and come back at once."

Darrell flew off. She came back with sou'westers. She had to put Bill's on for her, because Bill looked at the sou'wester as if she simply didn't know what it was.

"I'm going to phone now," said Miss Peters. "Walk him out, Bill."

She went. She telephoned the vet's house. The sleepy voice of his housekeeper answered her. "I'm sorry, Mam – but the vet has gone to Raglett's farm to a cow. He said he'd sleep there for the night. No, Mam – I'm afraid they're not on the telephone. You can't get the vet tonight. I'm sorry."

Miss Peters put down the receiver. Couldn't get the vet! What was to be done? The horse needed medicine, and only the vet could bring it and make him drink it down. Miss Peters cold see that Thunder's condition was serious. Something *must* be done!

She went out to the stables again. In the yard the two girls were walking Thunder round and round, the rain pouring down on them. She told them that the vet could not be reached. Bill groaned. She was in despair.

"He's at Raglett's farm," said Miss Peters. "That's

about five miles off, on the Billington Road. I know what I'll do. I'll saddle one of the other horses and ride to the farm myself and get him. That would be the best thing."

"What! In the dark and the rain?" said Darrell, hardly able to believe her ears.

"That's nothing," said Miss Peters. "Thunder is a lovely horse – I don't mind what I do for him."

Bill's hand groped for Miss Peters' arm. She was sobbing. "You *are* good!" she said. "Thank you, Miss Peters. You are the kindest person I've ever known. Oh, if only you can get the vet!"

Miss Peters patted Bill's shoulder. "I'll do my best. Don't worry, Bill!"

Darrell was struck with surprise. Miss Peters had called Bill Bill. Gracious! And she was going to ride for miles in the dark to fetch someone to help Thunder. She was a perfectly marvellous person! "And to think I never even guessed it before!" marvelled Darrell, valiantly leading Thunder round the yard. "People are awfully decent underneath."

Miss Peters was soon galloping off into the night. The two girls took it in turns to lead Thunder round the yard. He seemed better when he was walking.

"Darrell – I do feel so awful now to remember all the horrid things I thought about Miss Peters," said Bill, once. "She's the decentest person I've ever met. Fancy riding off like that to get the vet. Darrell, I shall never be able to repay her. Shall I?"

"No. I don't suppose you will," said Darrell. "I think she's fine. Golly – won't the girls be thrilled to hear about all this tomorrow!"

Miss Peters was riding fast through the night. The rain beat down on her but she didn't mind. She was an

122

all-weather person, and thought nothing of rain, wind, snow or fog! She galloped off to Raglett's farm, and at last got to the gate that led up to the farm.

There was a light in one of the sheds. Miss Peters guessed the vet was there with the farmer, and the cow he had gone to tend. She rode up to the door, her horse's hooves making a loud noise in the night.

The farmer came to the door in surprise. Miss Peters hailed him in her loud, deep voice. "Is the vet here? Can I speak to him?"

"He's in yonder," said the farmer. Miss Peters dismounted and went into the shed. The vet was there, kneeling beside a cow. By the cow's side were two pretty little calves.

"Mr Turnbull," said Miss Peters, "if you've finished here, could you possibly come to Malory Towers? That horse Thunder I told you about on the telephone this morning is in a bad way. Colic. He needs help."

"Right," said the vet, getting up. "I've finished here, as it happens – much earlier than I thought. I'll come along now. I'll get my horse. Well, Raglett, that cow's fine now – and she's got two of the prettiest calves I ever saw!"

Presently the vet and Miss Peters were riding back over the road to Malory Towers. When they were halfway there Miss Peters' horse suddenly shied and reared.

"Hey, there! Whoa! What's the matter?" cried Miss Peters – and at the same moment she saw something lying beside the road. It was a dark shape, hardly visible in the darkness of the night.

"Mr Turnbull. Come here!" yelled Miss Peters. "I think there's somebody here. I hope they haven't been

123

knocked down by a car and left helpless!"

The vet had a powerful torch. He switched it on. The beam played over a huddled up bundle – a bundle with a mackintosh on!

"Good heavens! It's a young girl!" said the vet. "Is she hurt?"

He picked the girl up. Miss Peters gave a loud and horrified exclamation. "It's MAVIS! Good gracious me! Mavis! Whatever is she doing lying out here in the dark at this time of night? This is terrible!"

"She's fainted from exhaustion I think," said the vet. "Doesn't seem to have any bones broken. Look, she's opening her eyes."

Mavis looked up and saw Miss Peters. She began to cry weakly. "They wouldn't let me sing. And I missed the last bus, and I've been walking all night in the rain."

"What *is* she talking about?" said the vet. "Look she's wet through! She'll get pneumonia unless we're pretty quick. I'll take her on my horse. Help me to lift her up."

Amazed, horrified and distressed, Miss Peters helped to lift Mavis on to the vet's horse. He held the girl steady in front of him. Then off they went again, this time more slowly.

They came to Malory Towers. "If Mavis can walk I'll take her straight in to Matron," said Miss Peters. "Oh dear, what a night! You go to the stables, Mr Turnbull. Darrell and Bill are walking Thunder in the yard."

The vet disappeared in the direction of the stables. Miss Peters guided the exhausted Mavis into North Tower. She could hardly walk. Miss Peters half-dragged her up the stairs to Matron's room.

"It's Mavis! Good gracious me!"

Matron awoke and opened the door in surprise. She exclaimed in horror when she saw Mavis. "What's all this? Where has she been? She's soaked through and shivering. Miss Peters, there's an electric blanket in that cupboard. Put it into the little bed over there, will you and get the bed hot. And put my electric kettle on. Good gracious! What can have happened?"

"Goodness knows," said Miss Peters, doing all the things she had been asked to do, whilst Matron quickly undressed Mavis, flinging her soaking clothes on the floor in her hurry to get her into a warm bed. It wasn't long before she was tucked up with two hot-water bottles, whilst Matron prepared some hot cocoa.

Mavis tried to tell her what had happened. She spoke in a poor croaking voice. "I only went to Billington – to that talent spotting concert – but they said they couldn't let schoolgirls enter. I tried and tried to make them let me sing, but they wouldn't. And then I missed the last bus so I began to walk all the way home. But it rained and blew and I was so tired I fell down. And I couldn't get up again. So . . ."

"Now, don't talk any more," said Matron, gently. "You drink this cocoa and go to sleep. I'll be here in this other bed so you'll be all right."

Miss Peters had slipped out of the room, murmuring something about seeing to a horse, much to Matron's surprise. She couldn't make out why Miss Peters was in riding things nor how it was that she had found Mavis on the road. Well, the main thing was to see to Mavis. She could find out the rest of the mystery afterwards.

Miss Peters went down to the others. Bill and Darrell had welcomed the vet with joy and relief.

Thunder knew him and whinnied. It wasn't long before the vet had made him drink a huge draught of medicine. "You've done well to keep him on his feet," he told the two tired girls. "Probably saved his life. Now – off you go to bed. I'll stay with him till morning. Miss Peters will help me. Off you go!"

Next Morning

Bill hadn't wanted to leave Thunder, of course. But Miss Peters spoke to her firmly and gently. "Now, Bill – you must leave matters to us. You know that we shall do our best for the horse, and now that he has had that draught he will be all right. We'll walk him as long as necessary. But you and Darrell have done your share and you are tired out. Be sensible, Bill, and do as you are told."

"Yes, I will," said Bill, unexpectedly. She took Miss Peters' hand in hers and held it tightly. "Miss Peters – I can never repay you. Never. But I'll never forget tonight and all you did."

Miss Peters patted Bill on the back. "That's all right. I'm not asking for any repayment! I'm fond of Thunder, too, and I knew how you felt. I'm not sending him home, Bill. You shall keep him. I don't somehow think I shall ever have to punish you again by saying you mustn't see him."

"You won't," said Bill, her face gleaming in the lamplight. "I'll be your – your very best pupil from now on, Miss Peters!"

"Well – that will be a wonderful repayment," said Miss Peters, smiling. "Now do go, both of you. You look so pale and tired. You must both have breakfast in bed!"

"Oh no!" protested both girls. "We couldn't bear it."

"All right. I can't bear it either," said Miss Peters. "You can go to bed early instead! Now, good night – or rather, good morning! It's nearly three o'clock!"

The two girls stumbled into North Tower, yawning. They hardly said a word to one another, they were so tired. But they were happy, and felt as if they had been friends for years! Bill slid into bed. She whispered to Darrell.

"Darrell! I know you're Sally's friend, so you can't be mine. But I'm yours for ever and ever. Just you remember that! I'll pay you back some day for all you did tonight."

"That's all right," said Darrell, sleepily, and was asleep almost at once.

In the morning, what a to-do! Darrell and Bill slept so soundly that not even the bell awoke them. When Jean pulled at them they shrugged away and cuddled down again, hardly waking.

"Darrell! Bill! I say, what's the matter with them both! Wake up, you two, the bell's gone ages ago. Do wake up – we want to tell you something. Mavis isn't back! Her bed is empty!"

The rest of the girls were talking excitedly about Mavis's non-appearance. Jean was very worried. She felt that she ought to have reported the night before that Mavis had not come to bed with the rest of them. She was feeling very guilty.

128

"I must go to Miss Potts at once," she said and she rushed off. But Miss Potts knew all about Mavis, for Matron had already reported to her. Miss Grayling knew, too. There had been a great upset about it. Mavis was now in the san. where sick girls were kept, and Sister, who looked after the san., was in charge of her. The doctor had been to see her already.

Jean listened to all this in amazement. "Did Mavis – did she go to Billington?" she asked.

"Oh! So you know about that too," said Miss Potts, grimly. "Funny sort of head girl you are, Jean, not to have reported that Mavis was not in the dormitory last night. Very remiss of you. There are times when you have to make a distinction between telling tales and reporting. You know that. We might have saved Mavis from a serious illness if we had learnt from you that she hadn't gone to bed."

Jean went white. "I fell asleep," she said, miserably, "I was going to wait till the last bus came in – and if Mavis didn't come in then I was going to come and report. But I fell asleep."

"A lame excuse," said Miss Potts, who was angry with herself for not having popped her head into the third form dormy the night before, when she had heard talking. If only she had!

"Can we see Mavis?" asked Jean.

"Certainly not," said Miss Potts. "She is seriously ill. She got soaked through, and then lay for some time by the roadside. She has bronchitis now – and we are hoping it won't turn to anything worse. Her throat is terribly bad, too – she can hardly whisper."

Jean went back to the third form dormy feeling guilty and alarmed. She found the third-formers gathered round Darrell, listening excitedly to her tale of the night before. Bill was not there. She had rushed off to the stables at once, of course.

"Listen . . ." said Jean. But nobody listened. They were all agape at Darrell's amazing tale. Jean found herself listening, too.

"But – would you believe Miss Peters could be so utterly decent?" said Belinda, in surprise. "She was super! How lucky that you fetched her, Darrell!"

"It *was* a night!" said Darrell. "Bill and I must have walked miles and miles with Thunder round the yard. I wonder how he is this morning."

Footsteps raced up the corridor to the dormy. Bill burst in, her face glowing. "Darrell! DARRELL! He's all right. Right as rain, and eating his oats as if he couldn't have enough. The vet stayed with him till half-past seven, and Miss Peters stayed till now. She never went to bed again!"

"Golly! She's wonderful," said Alicia, seeing Miss Peters in an entirely new light. "Bill, why didn't you and Darrell wake us up, too?"

"We never thought of anything like that," said Bill. "We only thought of Thunder. Darrell was marvellous, too. Oh, I feel so happy. Thunder's all right. He's not going to be sent home. Everything's fine. And I shall never, never forget what Miss Peters did last night."

"You will!" said Alicia. "You'll sit and look out of the window and dream in class, just as you always do!"

"I shan't," said Bill, earnestly. "Don't tease me, Alicia. I feel a bit strange though I feel so happy. Now I know that Miss Peters is fond of Thunder – and he loves her, too, fancy that! – I shall feel quite different about everything. I might even let her ride him."

Jean at last got a word in. "Listen to *me* now!" she

said, and she told the third-formers about Mavis. They listened in horrified silence. Darrell burst out at once.

"Gracious! So Miss Peters didn't only save Thunder last night – she saved Mavis, too. But I say – fancy Mavis trying to walk home all those miles in the dark by herself. She's afraid of the dark, too."

The girls were happy about Bill and Thunder, but upset about Mavis. They stood about in the dormy, talking, forgetting all about breakfast. Somebody came running up the corridor. It was Lucy of the fourth form.

"I *say*! What are you all thinking of? Aren't you coming to breakfast? The bell's gone long ago, and Mam'zelle is absolutely furious!"

"Oh dear! Come on, everyone," said Jean. "I feel all in a whirl."

The news about Thunder and about Mavis spread all through the school, and was the talk in every class from the bottom form to the top. Darrell and Bill had to tell the tale over and over again.

It was Sunday so there were no classes. In the school chapel, where the service was held, a prayer was said for Mavis. All the girls joined in it, for although few of them liked Mavis they were all sorry for her. The news went round that she was worse. Her parents had been sent for! Oh dear, thought Jean, it was all her fault!

By the next morning, however, Mavis had taken a turn for the better. Thunder, too, was perfectly all right. Bill was thrilled. It seemed impossible that a horse in such pain as Thunder had been should be quite recovered the day after. How wonderful people like doctors and vets were!

The girls settled down to their classes on Monday,

glad that Mavis was better. Jean especially was thankful. Perhaps she would soon be back in school. The whole matter would have blown over. Mavis would be given a talking to by Miss Grayling, but no punishment because she had punished herself enough. Everything would be all right.

Miss Peters had had a good rest on the Sunday, and was taking the third form as usual on Monday. When she came into the classroom, she had a surprise.

"Hurrah for Miss Peters!" cried Darrell's voice and to the amazement of the forms on each side of the third form room, three hearty cheers rang out for Miss Peters. She couldn't help being pleased. She smiled pleasantly all round.

"Thank you," she said. "That was nice of you. Now – open your books at page forty-three. Alicia, come up to the blackboard, please."

Darrell looked with interest at Bill several times that morning. Bill didn't gaze out of the window once. She paid great attention to every word that Miss Peters said. She answered intelligently, and when it was her turn to come up to the blackboard, she did extremely well.

"Very good, Bill," said Miss Peters, and a gasp went round the class. Miss Peters hadn't called her Wilhelmina as she always did. She had called her Bill. Bill grinned as she went back to her place. She looked a different person.

Darrell admired her as she watched her in class after class. Bill had made up her mind to do a thing and she meant to do it. She *would* do it, too! Darrell thought that it was quite possible for Bill to rise near the top of the class once she had made up her mind to do it.

"I suppose that's what Daddy would call strength of

132

character," thought Darrell. "He's always saying that strength of character is one of the greatest things anyone can have because then they have courage and pluck and determination, no matter what difficulties come. Bill's got it. I bet she won't dream, or gaze out of the window again, or not bother with her work. She's going to repay Miss Peters for Saturday night!"

Miss Peters knew that Bill meant to repay her for that, too. She trusted Bill now. They understood one another, which really wasn't very surprising, because they were very much alike. Miss Peters was mannish, and Bill was boyish. They both loved life out-of-doors and adored horses. They had disliked one another very much indeed – but now they were going to be firm friends. That would be nice for Bill.

"Darrell! Are you daydreaming?" said Miss Peters' voice. "You don't seem to have written down anything at all!"

Darrell jumped and went red. Gracious! Here she was admiring Bill for being able to stop dreaming in class – and she, Darrell, had fallen into the same fault herself! She pulled herself together and began to write.

That afternoon Miss Hibbert was going to take the first rehearsal of the play in the art room. This was often used for dramatic work because it had a small platform. Zerelda was very much looking forward to the afternoon. She sat in her place, murmuring some lines from "Romeo and Juliet" below her breath. Miss Peters saw her lips moving and thought she was whispering to Gwen.

"Zerelda!" she said sharply. "What are you saying to Gwendoline?"

"Nothing, Miss Peters," said Zerelda, surprised.

"Well, what were you saying to yourself then?"

demanded Miss Peters. "Stand up when you answer me, Zerelda."

Zerelda stood up. She looked at Miss Peters and recited dramatically what she had been murmuring to herself.

> "Wilt thou be gone? It is not yet near day;
> It was the nightingale and not . . ."

A volley of laughter from everyone in the class drowned her voice. Miss Peters rapped sharply on her desk.

"Zerelda! I hope you don't really *mean* to be rude. That's enough! We are doing geography, not Shakespeare. Sit down and get on!"

At the Rehearsal

After the dinner hour that day the third-formers brought up the subject of Alicia's trick again.

"You know, Alicia – I don't somehow feel as if I want it played on Miss Peters now," said Bill.

"Nor do I," said Darrell.

"I don't want it played at all," said Sally, stoutly.

"Well, you're the only one that doesn't," said Alicia. "So keep quiet. What does everyone else say?"

"*I* don't quite like to play it on Miss Peters now," said Belinda. "I feel like Bill and Darrell. You know – it seems a bit odd to give three cheers for somebody

134

and then the very next day play a trick on them like that."

"*I* shouldn't mind," said Zerelda, who hadn't liked being ticked off in class that morning by Miss Peters. "What's in a trick, anyway? Only a bit of fun. I guess it wouldn't matter at all."

"I agree with Zerelda," said Gwen's voice. "Why shouldn't we? Don't you agree, Daphne?"

"I don't know," said Daphne, who had been rather struck with Miss Peters' dramatic ride through the night. "No – I think on the whole I'd rather play it on Mam'zelle – or Miss Carton, perhaps."

"Well, I don't much care who we play it on," said Alicia. "Darrell and I will agree to what the majority say."

"Darrell and you!" exclaimed Sally. "What's Darrell got to do with it? It's *your* trick, not hers!"

"Oh, we've just been planning it out together that's all," said Alicia, coolly, pleased to see Sally's jealousy flare up in public. Darrell went red. It was true she had enjoyed talking over the trick with Alicia – but she knew quite well that Alicia was only saying that to make Sally cross. Bother them both! Why couldn't they all be friends together? Never mind – Betty was coming back soon. Then perhaps Alicia would stop teasing Sally and Sally would stop being jealous and spiteful.

"Well – let's play the trick on Mam'zelle then," said Irene. "Mam'zelle's lovely to play tricks on. We haven't played one on her for terms and terms."

"Right. Mam'zelle it shall be," said Alicia. "Do you agree, Darrell? We'll talk about the best time and so on together when we've got a minute to ourselves. It's time to get over to the art room now."

They all went off to the art room, Sally looking glum. Alicia slipped her arm in Darrell's and bore her off as if she really was her best friend. Darrell glanced back at Sally and tried to take her arm away from Alicia. But Sally gave her such a sour look that Darrell was annoyed, and didn't go back to her after all.

Privately Darrell thought the hour of Shakespeare was a dreadful waste, because it was a fine sunny afternoon when a game of lacrosse could have been arranged. Still it would be fun to see Zerelda trying to impress Miss Hibbert.

Zerelda was excited. This was her great chance. If only she could bring it off – make Miss Hibbert say what a gift for acting she had. "Zerelda, you're a born actress!" she would say to her. "You have a great gift. You must turn all your attention to building it up. You have the right appearance, too – striking, graceful, mature. It will make me very proud to teach you this year!"

Zerelda had done a little roll of hair on top of her head again – not so big a roll as before, certainly, but still a roll, pinned up to make her look older. Her hair was not tied back so tightly either. She had made up her face a little – put red on her lips, pink on her cheeks, and had smothered herself with powder. Her hands were white. Her nails were very long and highly polished. She hoped she looked a finished actress!

Miss Hibbert did not look at all like a producer of plays. She was neat, with a well-fitting coat and skirt, and her hair, slightly wavy, was brushed well back. She wore a pair of glasses with rather thick rims. She was very efficient, and knew exactly how to pick the right actor for the right part.

She looked over the girls as they came in. She knew

Zerelda already because she had taken her for a few lessons in the fourth form. She looked in astonishment at Zerelda's make-up. Good gracious! What did the girl think she was up to!

Miss Hibbert had absolutely no idea at all that Zerelda fancied herself as an actress or as a film star. Nobody had told her. Perhaps if she had known, she might have been a little more patient, even a little kinder. But she didn't know.

There was a lot to get through. For one reason or another two rehearsals had been put off, and Miss Hibbert was feeling a little rushed for time. She handed out copies of the play and looked round the form.

"Now – has anyone acted in this play before?"

Nobody had. Zerelda stepped forward and said a few words, trying to speak the English way. "Please, Miss Hibbert, once I did Lady Macbeth, in Shakespeare."

"Oh," said Miss Hibbert, gazing at Zerelda's hair. "Zerelda, I don't like the way you do your hair. Don't come to my classes with that silly roll on top again."

Zerelda went red and stepped back.

"Has anyone read the play?" Darrell and Mary-Lou put up their hands, and so did Zerelda.

"Does anyone know any of the parts? Has anyone been sufficiently interested to learn any of the speeches?" went on Miss Hibbert.

Zerelda stepped forward again. "Please, Miss Hibbert, I know all Juliet's speeches, every one of them. I guess I could say them all, right now. It's a wunnerful part, Juliet's. I've been rehearsing it like mad."

"Yes. She's awfully good as Juliet," put in Gwendoline, and got a grateful smile from Zerelda.

137

"Very well. As you've taken the trouble to learn the part, you can take it this afternoon," said Miss Hibbert. She looked round the class for a boyish third-former to take the part of Romeo. Her eye fell on Bill.

"You," she said. "What's your name – Wilhelmina – you can take the part of Romeo today. And you, Darrell, can be the nurse, and you . . ."

Quickly she fitted part after part. The girls looked at their copies of the play and prepared to read and act them.

"Not very inspired," said Miss Hibbert, after the first few pages had been read. "Turn to the part where Juliet comes on. Zerelda, are you ready?"

Was she *ready*? Why, she was waiting on tenterhooks to begin! She was full of it! She was Juliet to the life, poor, tragic Juliet.

Zerelda launched herself into the part. She declaimed her lines in a most dramatic manner, she flung herself about, she marched up and down, she threw her head back, imagining herself to be beautiful and most lovable.

"Stop, Zerelda," said Miss Hibbert, amazed. But Zerelda didn't stop. Heedless of the giggles of the class she ranted on. Irene gave one of her enormous snorts, and Miss Hibbert glared at her. She spoke loudly to Zerelda again.

"STOP, Zerelda!"

Zerelda stopped and stared blankly at Miss Hibbert, surprised to see that she looked so furious.

"How dare you behave like that?" stormed Miss Hibbert. "Sending the class into fits! Do you think that's the way to behave in a Shakespeare class? They may think it comical but I don't. Those are lovely lines

138

you have been saying – but you have completely spoilt them. And do you really think it is clever to throw yourself about like that, and toss your head? Don't you know that Juliet was young and gentle and sweet? You are trying to make her into some horrible affected film star!"

Zerelda took in what the angry mistress was saying. She could hardly believe it. She went rather white under the pink of her cheeks.

"And why have you made yourself up like that?" demanded Miss Hibbert, roused to more anger by the giggles of the rest of the form. "I cannot tell you how horrible you look with that stuff on your face. You would not dare to go to Miss Peters' class like that. I'm not going to put up with it. You may as well make up your mind, Zerelda, that you will never be an actress. You simply haven't got it in you. All that happens is that you make yourself really vulgar. Now go and wash your face and do your hair properly."

Zerelda felt like a balloon that had been pricked. All her confidence and pride oozed out of her. She crept to the door and went out. Some of the girls felt sorry for her.

Rather subdued by this unusual outburst, the rest of the form went on reading. Miss Hibbert, a little sorry that she had been so very hard on Zerelda, handed out a few words of praise. "Alicia, you're good. Mary-Lou, you have a nice voice if you could remember to hold your head up when you speak your lines. Darrell, I can see you are trying. Next time we will all take different parts."

"Miss Hibbert, had I better go and see what has happened to Zerelda?" asked Gwen, timidly. "Miss Hibbert, she really did think she had a gift for acting,

139

you know. Aren't you going to to let her be in the play at all?"

"I may give her a very small part – where she can't throw herself about," said Miss Hibbert. "But certainly not a good part. It must be obvious even to you, Gwendoline, that Zerelda hasn't got the faintest idea of acting, and never will have. Go and find her and tell her to come here to me. I want to talk to her. The class is now dismissed."

The third-formers went out quietly. Poor Zerelda! What would she do now?

"Put a bold face on it, I expect," said Alicia. "Just as she did when she was sent down to the third form. She won't care! She'll go on in just the same way, thinking the world of herself, and very little of anyone else!"

Zerelda was found by Gwen in the cloakroom. She had washed her face quite clean and tied back her hair. But she had been too scared to go back to the art room.

"Zerelda, Miss Hibbert wants you," said Gwen. "I'm sorry about that row. It's a shame."

"*Can't* I act, Gwen?" said Zerelda, her lip quivering suddenly. Gwendoline hesitated.

"Well – you weren't very good really," she said. "You – you just seemed to be terribly funny. You might make a very good *comedian*, Zerelda."

Zerelda said nothing but went off to the art room. Even Gwen thought she couldn't act! In fact, she was so bad that she became ridiculous. Zerelda was shocked and dismayed. She dreaded hearing what Miss Hibbert had to say.

But Miss Hibbert was unexpectedly kind. "I hear that it is your ambition to be a great actress, Zerelda," she said. "Well, my dear, it is given to very few of us

140

to be that. You haven't the gift – and you haven't another thing that all really fine actresses need."

"What?" whispered Zerelda.

"Well, Zerelda, in order to be able to put yourself properly into some other character, you have to forget yourself entirely – forget your looks, your ambitions, your pride in acting, everything! And it takes a strong and understanding character to do that, someone without conceit or weakness of any sort – the finer the character of the actor, the better he can play any part. You are thinking of yourself too much. You were not Juliet being acted by Zerelda this afternoon – you were Zerelda all the time – and not a very nice Zerelda either!"

"Shan't I ever be any good at acting?" asked Zerelda, miserably.

"I don't think so," said Miss Hibbert, gently. "I can always tell at once those who have any gift for it. You have let your foolish worship and admiration of the film stars blind you, Zerelda. Why not try to be your own self for a while? Stop all this posturing and pretending. Be like the others, a schoolgirl sent here to learn lessons and play games!"

"It's the only thing left for me to be," said Zerelda, and a tear ran down her cheek.

"It's a very, very *nice* thing to be," said Miss Hibbert. "You try it and see! I wouldn't have been so hard on you if I'd known you had set your heart on being an actress. I thought you were just being ridiculous."

Zerelda left the art room, hardly knowing what to think. She had made herself ridiculous. She never, never wanted to act again! All she wanted to do was to sink into being a nobody, hoping that none of the others would notice her and tease her about that afternoon.

She joined the others for tea, slipping into her place unnoticed by the girls. Miss Potts looked at her and saw that she had been crying. "Funny thing!" thought Miss Potts, "it's the first time I've noticed it, but Zerelda is getting to look much more like the others now – a proper little schoolgirl. Perhaps Malory Towers is beginning to have an effect after all!"

The Trick!

One or two days slipped by. Mavis was still very ill and could not be seen, but it was known now that she was mending. Everyone was relieved. The girls sent in flowers and books, and Zerelda sent her a complicated American jigsaw.

Bill had quite recovered from her midnight adventure and so had Darrell. Miss Peters was delighted with the change in Bill's work. It was still uneven, but she knew that Bill was paying great attention and really trying hard. Zerelda, too, was working even better, and had actually asked Mam'zelle for extra coaching!

Zerelda had sorted things out in her mind. She had definitely given up the idea of becoming a film actress. She didn't even want to *look* like one! She wanted to look as like the others as possible, and to make them forget how ridiculous she had been. She began to copy them in every way she could.

"Isn't Zerelda strange?" said Belinda to Irene. "When she first came here she gave herself such airs and graces, and looked down on the whole lot of us – now she tries to copy us in everything – the way we speak, the way we do this and that – and seems to think we're just 'wunnerful'!"

"She's much nicer," said Irene, trying out the rhythm of a tune on the table in front of her. "Tum-tum-ti-tum. Yes, that's how it goes. I like Zerelda now, really I do."

"Look – Gwendoline's scowling again!" said Belinda, in a whisper. "I can get that scowl this time. Isn't it a beauty?"

Gwen suddenly became aware of Belinda's intent glances. She straightened her face at once. "If you've drawn me, I'll tear up the paper!" she said.

"Oh, *Gwen* – scowl half a minute more and I'll get it!" begged Belinda. But Gwen walked out of the room, putting the scowl on outside the door because she felt so annoyed with Belinda and her impish pencil.

"About that trick," said Alicia, suddenly to Darrell. "Shall we play it on Friday? Mam'zelle was murmuring this morning something about a test then."

"Oh *yes*. Let's!" said Darrell, thrilled. She saw Sally nearby, her face glum. "Sally! Do say you agree. It really will be funny – and quite harmless."

"I've said already I'm not going to have anything to do with the trick," said Sally. "I think it's a silly trick, and might be dangerous. I can't see how anyone can sneeze and sneeze without feeling exhausted. Do it if you like – but just remember that I don't agree!"

"Spoilsport," said Alicia, in a low voice to Darrell. Darrell sighed. She couldn't back out of the trick now just to please Sally – but she did hate it when Sally wouldn't be friends. Never mind – Betty would be coming back this week. On Friday perhaps! Then Alicia wouldn't bother about her anymore. Betty had been away for more than six weeks now – it was past half term – but she had been sent away to the seaside, after her whooping cough was over, because she had had it so badly. Good gracious – there were only three or four weeks to the end of the term! How the time had flown. It was March now, and the early daffodils were blowing in the courtyard.

Alicia and Darrell made their plans. "We'll put the little pellet, soaked in salt water, on the little ledge behind Mam'zelle," said Alicia. "Let's see – who's on duty to get the room ready on Friday? Oh, I do believe it's you, isn't it, Darrell? That will be easy then. You can put the pellet there yourself."

"Yes, I will," agreed Darrell, beginning to giggle at the thought of Mam'zelle's surprise when she kept sneezing.

All the third-formers knew about the joke. Only Sally disapproved. Jean didn't think there was any harm in it at all, so she didn't draw back either. Everyone was thrilled at the thought of Friday.

It came at last. Darrell slipped into the form room with the little pellet and a sponge soaked in salt water. She set the pellet on the ledge and squeezed a few drops of water from the sponge over it. That was apparently all that was needed to make it work.

The others came in to get ready for the class. They raised their eyebrows at Darrell, and she nodded back, smiling. They all took their places, ready for

Mam'zelle.

She came in, beaming as usual. "*Asseyez-vous, mes enfants*. Today we have a great, great treat. It is a test!"

Deep groans from the class.

"Silence!" hissed Mam'zelle. "Do you want Miss Potts to come and find out what is the meaning of this terrible noise? Now, I will write some questions on the blackboard, and you will answer them in your books."

She turned to write on the blackboard, and got the first whiff of the fine vapour, quite invisible, that was streaming from the curious little pellet.

Mam'zelle felt a tickling in her nose, and felt about her plump person for her handkerchief. "Ah, where is it, now? I have a nose-tickle."

"Your hanky's in your belt, Mam'zelle," called Alicia, hoping that Irene wasn't going to do one of her explosions too soon. She already looked as if she was on the point of bursting.

Mam'zelle also looked as if she was bursting. She snatched at her handkerchief and pressed it to her nose. But no handkerchief could choke down that colossal sneeze. Mam'zelle always did sneeze loudly at any time – but this time it sounded like an explosive shell!

"A-WHOOSH-OOOO! Dear me," said Mam'zelle, patting her nose with her handkerchief. "I'm sorry girls, I could not help it."

Irene had already bent down to hide her giggles under the desk. Alicia glanced at her in amused annoyance. Whatever would she do when Mam'zelle's second sneeze came along. Ah – it was coming. Mam'zelle was making a frantic grab for her handkerchief again.

"Oh, *là là*! Here is another snizz. I hope I do not get a cold. A-WHOOOSH-OOOOOOO!"

Irene exploded and so did Belinda. Mam'zelle, quite shaken by her enormous sneeze, glared at them both.

"Irene! Belinda! It is not kind to laugh at another's discom. . . A-WHOOOSH-OO!"

But now even Alicia could not hide her laughter. Darrell leaned back weakly and tried to stop laughing because her side ached so much. Even Sally was smiling, though she tried hard not to.

"A-WHOOOSH-OOO!" sneezed Mam'zelle again. She reeled back to her chair, and mopped her forehead. "Never have I snizzed like this before," she said. "It is unheard of that I snizz so much. A-WHOOOOSH-OOOOOO!"

The last one was so terrific that it shook poor Mam'zelle right out of her chair. By now the whole class was in convulsions. Gwen was falling out of her chair. In another moment Irene would be rolling on the floor. Tears of laughter were pouring down the cheeks of half a dozen of the girls.

Mam'zelle sat staring at the blackboard wondering if the sneezing had finished. Perhaps the attack was over. She got up cautiously and went to the blackboard – but at once her nose began to tickle again and she put up her handkerchief. "A-WHOOOO -SH-OOO!"

Mam'zelle sank down into her chair again. At this moment the door opened and Miss Potts looked in with a sheaf of papers. "Oh, excuse me, Mam'zelle, but you left these . . ." she began, and then stopped short in surprise at seeing the whole form rolling about in helpless laughter. Whatever was happening?

She looked at Mam'zelle, and Mam'zelle looked

"A-tish-oo!" sneezed poor Miss Potts

back, trying to tell her what was happening. Another exploding sneeze nearly blew Miss Potts out of the door.

"A-WHOOOSH-OOOOOO!"

The class sobered up when they saw Miss Potts. They hoped she would go immediately – but she didn't. Rather alarmed at Mam'zelle's agonized expression, she went over to her. "It is these snizzes – " Mam'zelle began to explain and was then overcome by another.

The vapour found its way to Miss Potts' nose. She was just about to open her mouth to speak when she too felt a sneeze coming. Her nose began to tickle and she felt for her handkerchief.

"A-TISH-OOO!" she sneezed, and Irene burst into one of her explosive laughs at once. Miss Potts glared at her.

"Irene! Do you think. . . A-TISH-OOOO!"

"A-WHOOOOSH-OOOOOO!" from Mam'zelle. "Miss Potts what is this snizzing? I cannot stop my snizzes – A-WHOOOSH-OO!"

Miss Potts sneezed three times without being able to get a word in between the sneezes. Then a sudden suspicion flashed into her mind. She looked at the giggling girls.

"Jean," she said, "you are head girl of this form. Is this a trick? A-TISH-OO!"

Jean hesitated. How could she give the whole form away?

Mam'zelle saved her from further questioning. She sneezed such a mighty sneeze that she fell off her chair. She moaned. "I am ill! I have never snizzed like this before. I am very ill. A-WHOOOOSH-OO."

Really alarmed, Miss Potts, hindered by two or

three sudden sneezes of her own, dragged Mam'zelle to her feet. "Open the window," she commanded Darrell. "Fetch Matron. Mam'zelle certainly does look ill."

In great alarm Darrell opened the window and Mary-Lou ran for Matron. Matron came, puzzled by Mary-Lou's breathless tale of Mam'zelle's sneezes. She saw Mam'zelle's pale face and took her arm to lead her away. The pellet-vapour overtook Matron also, and she did a very sudden sneeze indeed. Miss Potts also obliged with two more, and Mam'zelle prepared for yet another. Then Matron took Mam'zelle from the room, and Miss Potts followed, to make sure poor Mam'zelle was all right.

The girls, alarmed and frightened though they were, could not help from laughing at the sight of the three adults sneezing in chorus together. "You were nearly caught out with Miss Potts' question, Jean," said Alicia. "It was a narrow shave! Let's hope she doesn't ask it again."

"I hope Mam'zelle isn't *really* knocked out," said Darrell, anxiously. "She did look rather awful. I think I'll quickly take that pellet and throw it out of the window before Miss Potts comes back and sees it!"

So she threw it out, being caught for a sneeze herself first. Then the form settled down to wait for someone to come back.

It was Miss Potts. "Mam'zelle is not at all well," she began, severely, handkerchief in hand in case she began to sneeze again. "She has had to go to bed. She is quite exhausted. The strange – very strange – thing is, that as soon as we left this room not one of us had any wish to sneeze. Jean, will you please explain this to me. Or perhaps you, Alicia, would like to do so? I feel

149

that you probably know more about it than anyone else."

Alicia hardly knew what to say. Jean nudged her. "Go on. You'll have to tell."

So Alicia told. It didn't seem nearly such a funny idea when it was told stammeringly to a frowning Miss Potts.

"I see. One of your asinine tricks again. I should have thought that third-formers were above such childish things. Were you all in this, every one of you?"

"Sally wasn't," said Darrell. "She refused to agree. She was the only one who stood out."

"Only one sensible person in the whole of the form!" said Miss Potts. "Very well – with the exception of Sally, each of you will forfeit the next half-holiday, which is, I believe, on Thursday. You will also apologize to Mam'zelle and work twice as hard at your French for the rest of the term!"

Mavis and Zerelda

It was a sorry ending to what everyone had thought to be a very fine trick. "I suppose that pellet had been made stronger than usual," said Alicia, gloomily.

Sally didn't say "I told you so" which was very good of her, Darrell thought. "I shall give up the half-holiday just the same as you all do," she told Darrell. "I may have stood out against the trick, but I'm going to share the punishment, of course."

"You're decent, Sally," said Darrell, slipping her arm in hers. "Let's go downstairs and see if there's anything interesting on the notice board. I believe there's a debate tonight we might go to – sixth-formers against fifth-formers, all arguing their heads off."

They went to find the notice board. One of the fourth-formers was also there, looking at it. It was Ellen. "Hallo, Darrell!" she said. "Congratulations!"

"What on?" asked Darrell, surprised.

"Well, look – you're playing for the third match-team next Thursday!" said Ellen. "Three people have fallen out, ill – so all three reserves are playing – and you're one of them, aren't you?"

"Oh – how perfectly wizard!" cried Darrell. She capered round the hall – and then her face suddenly sobered. "I say – will Miss Potts let me play next Thursday? That's the half-holiday, isn't it, except for match-players? Oh, Sally – do you think I shan't be able to play because we've all got to give up our half-holiday and work instead?'

"What *are* you talking about?" said Ellen, puzzled. Darrell told her.

"Goodness!" said Ellen. "You won't be able to play then. You can't expect Potty to let you off a punishment in order to have a great treat like playing in a match-team."

Darrell groaned. "Oh – what simply awful bad luck. My first chance! And I've chucked it away. Oh, Sally, why didn't I back you up and stand aside with you, instead of going in with Alicia?"

It was a terrible blow to poor Darrell. She went about looking so miserable that Sally couldn't bear it. She went to Miss Potts' room and knocked at the door.

"Please, Miss Potts – Darrell is down to play in the third match-team next Thursday," said Sally. "And because of the trick today she's supposed to work on that day. She's terribly disappointed. You said I needn't give up the half-holiday because I didn't agree to the trick. Can I give it up, please, and let Darrell take it instead of me? Then she could play in the match."

"A kind thought, Sally, but quite impossible," said Miss Potts. "Darrell must take her punishment like the rest of the form. It's her own fault if she misses her chance of playing in the match."

Sally went away sadly. She met Darrell and told her how she had tried to get her the half-holiday so that she might play in the team. Darrell was touched. "Oh, Sally! You really *are* a sport! A proper friend! Thank you."

Sally smiled at her. Her jealousy slid away suddenly. She knew she had been silly, but she wouldn't be anymore. She linked her arm in Darrell's.

"I'll be glad when Betty's back and Alicia has her for company," she said.

"So will I," said Darrell, heartily. "It's annoying the way she keeps trying to make us into a threesome. Don't let's, Sally."

Sally was satisfied. But how she wished she could give Darrell her half-holiday! Poor Darrell – it was such a wonderful chance – one that might not come again for ages.

They met Sister and asked her for news of Mavis. "Much better," said Sister. "Her *voice* has gone though. She can only croak, poor Mavis. She seems very miserable. She can have a visitor tomorrow. She's asked for Zerelda, so you might tell her she can go to see Mavis after tea."

Darrell and Sally looked at each other in astonishment. Zerelda! Whatever did Mavis want Zerelda for?

Mavis was very unhappy. She had been horrified when she found that her voice had gone. She had only a croak that sounded quite unlike her own voice. "Oh, Sister – won't I ever be able to sing again?" she had asked, anxiously.

"Not for some time," Sister had said. "Oh, yes, I expect it will come back all right, Mavis – but you have been very ill with throat and chest trouble, and you won't have to try and sing for a year or two. If you do the specialist says you will damage your voice for ever, and will never be able to become a singer."

Mavis let the tears slide down her cheeks without wiping them away. No voice! No singing for a year or two – and perhaps not then. Why, she might not become an opera singer after all. Throat trouble – chest trouble – they were the two things a singer must always guard against.

"It's my own fault! Why did I creep off in the rain that night?" wept poor Mavis. "I thought it was a grand thing to do. The others didn't. Perhaps Zerelda would understand though – she's going to be a grand film actress, and she understands how a singer or an actress longs to be recognized, aches for applause."

So, when Sister told her she could have a visitor and asked her whom she would like, she chose Zerelda! She must tell Zerelda everything. Zerelda would understand and sympathize.

Zerelda was surprised, too, to be chosen. She hadn't liked Mavis very much. But she went to see her, taking some fruit, some sweets and a book that had just come for her from America. Zerelda was always

153

generous.

She was shocked to see how thin Mavis looked. "Sit down," said Mavis, in a terrible croak.

"What's happened to your voice?" asked Zerelda, in alarm.

"I've lost it – perhaps for ever!" said Mavis, in a pathetic croak. "Oh, Zerelda, I've been an idiot. I'm sure nobody would understand but you!'

In a series of pants and croaks she told Zerelda all the happenings of that Saturday night – and how they wouldn't even *let* her sing. "So it was all for nothing. Oh, Zerelda, what am I to do without my voice? I shall die! The others have always told me that I'm nothing without my voice, nothing at all."

"Don't talk any more, Mavis," said Sister, putting her head in at the door. "You talk instead, Zerelda."

So Zerelda talked. What did she find to talk about? Ah, Zerelda suddenly found a bit of character and quite a lot of wisdom. She had learnt quite a few things already from her term at Malory Towers – she had especially learnt from her failure at acting. And she told Mavis all she had learnt.

It wasn't easy to tell what had happened in the Shakespeare class – but when Zerelda saw how Mavis was drinking it all in, paying her the very closest attention, she spared herself nothing.

"So you see, Mavis," she finished at last, "I was much, much worse than you. You really *had* a gift. I never had! You were proud of a real thing. I was vain of something false, that didn't exist. I'm happier now I know, though. After all, it *is* more sensible to be what we really are, isn't it – schoolgirls – not future film actresses or opera singers. You'll feel the same, too, when you've thought about it. You can be *you* now you've lost your voice for a bit."

"Oh, Zerelda," croaked Mavis, slipping her hand into the American girl's, "you don't know how you've helped me. I was so terribly miserable. I didn't think anything like this had ever happened to anyone before. And it's happened to *you* as well as to me!"

Zerelda said nothing. It had cost her a lot to make such a confession to Mavis, of all people. But with all her faults, Zerelda was generous-hearted, and she had quickly seen how she, and she alone, could help Mavis.

Sister put her head in again. She was glad to see Mavis looking so much happier. She came right in. "Well, you *have* done her good, Zerelda!" she said. "She looks quite different. You're friends, I suppose?"

Mavis looked eagerly at Zerelda. "Yes," said Zerelda firmly. "We're friends."

"Well, two minutes more and you must go," said Sister and went out again.

"I'm going to make the others see that I wasn't only a voice," croaked Mavis. "Zerelda, will you go on helping me? Will you be friends with me? I'm not much, I know – but you haven't got a friend, have you?"

"No," said Zerelda, ashamed to say it. "Well – I suppose I'm not much of a person either, Mavis. I'm just a no-account person – both of us are! We'll help each other. Now I must go. Goodbye! I'll come again tomorrow."

155

Things Get Straightened Out

Mam'zelle soon recovered from her fit of "snizzes", and returned to her teaching the next day. At first she had felt very angry when Miss Potts had explained to her that it was all because of some trick the girls had played.

But gradually her sense of humour came back to her and she found herself chuckling when she thought of Miss Potts and Matron also being caught by the trick and sneezing violently too.

"But I had the greatest snizzes," said Mam'zelle to herself. "Aha – here is Mam'zelle Rougier. I will tell her of this trick."

She told the prim, rather sour-faced Mam'zelle Rougier who did not approve of tricks in any shape or form. She was horrified.

"These English girls! Have you told Miss Grayling? They should all be punished, every one."

"Oh *no* – I haven't reported them to the Head," said Mam'zelle Dupont. "I only do that for serious matters."

"And you do not call this a serious matter!" cried Mam'zelle Rougier. "You will overlook it, and not have the girls punished at all! That Alicia – and the mad Irene and the bad Belinda – it would do them good to have a hard punishment."

"Oh, they are all being punished," said Mam'zelle,

156

hastily. "They are to give up their half-holiday, and work instead."

"That is no real punishment!" said Mam'zelle Rougier. "You are poor at discipline, Mam'zelle Dupont. I have always said so."

"Indeed, I am not!" cried Mam'zelle Dupont, annoyed. "Have you no sense of humour? Do you not see the funny side?"

"No, I do not," said Mam'zelle Rougier, firmly. "What is this 'funny side' that the English speak of so much? It is not funny. You too know that it is not, Mam'zelle."

The more that Mam'zelle Rougier talked like this the more certain Mam'zelle Dupont was that the joke had been funny. In the end she quite persuaded herself that she had really entered into it and laughed with the girls.

She almost felt that she would like to remove the punishment Miss Potts had imposed. But Miss Potts would not hear of it. "Certainly not! Don't be weak, Mam'zelle. We can't possibly let things like that pass."

"Perhaps not," said Mam'zelle, a sudden idea coming into her head. "The bad girls! They shall come to me for the whole of Thursday afternoon, Miss Potts, and I will make them WORK."

"That's better," said Miss Potts, approvingly. She found Mam'zelle very difficult at times. "Keep them at it all the afternoon!"

"I shall take them for a walk," thought Mam'zelle. She hated walks herself, but she knew how much the girls loved them. But when Thursday afternoon came, it was such a pouring wet day that not only was no lacrosse match possible but no walk either.

Darrell saw a notice up on the board beside the list of players. "MATCH CANCELLED. ANOTHER DATE WILL BE FIXED LATER."

"Look at that!" she said to Sally. "No match after all. How frightfully disappointed I'd have been if I'd been playing – and it was cancelled. I wonder if there's any hope of my playing on the next date it's arranged. I suppose the girls who are ill will be better by then, though."

The girls went to their classroom that afternoon, to work, while all the other forms went down to the big hall to play mad games together, and to see a film afterwards on a big screen put up at the end of the hall.

Mam'zelle was waiting for them, a broad smile on her face. "Poor children! You have to work this afternoon because of my snizzes. You must learn some French dances. I have brought my gramophone and some records. I will teach you a fine country dance that all French children know."

In surprise and glee the third-formers put back all the desks and chairs. They hoped Miss Potts would come by, or Miss Peters, and see what kind of work they were doing on their forfeited half-holiday! What sport to see their faces if they looked into the room!

But Mam'zelle had made sure that both these mistresses would not come that way. Miss Peters had gone off for the afternoon. Miss Potts would be in the big hall with her first form. Mam'zelle was safe!

"The coast is bright!" said Mam'zelle, gleefully. The girls giggled.

"You mean, 'the coast is *clear*,'" said Jean.

"It is the same thing," said Mam'zelle. "Now – begin! Form a ring, please, and I will tell you what to sing as you go round to the music."

It was a hilarious afternoon, and the third-formers enjoyed it very much. "You're a sport, Mam'zelle," said Darrell, warmly, at the end. "A real sport."

Mam'zelle beamed. She had never yet been able to understand exactly what a "sport" was – she only knew it was very high praise, and she was pleased.

"You made me snizz – and I have made you pant!" she said, to the breathless girls. "We are evens, are we not?"

"Quits, you mean," said Jean, but Mam'zelle took no notice.

"I shall tell Miss Potts you have quite exhausted yourselves in your hard work this afternoon," said Mam'zelle. "Poor children – you will be so hungry for tea!"

Zerelda had enjoyed herself as much as anyone. In fact, she was very surprised to find how much she had enjoyed the whole afternoon. Why – a week ago she would have turned up her nose at such rowdiness, and would only have joined in languidly, pretending it was all beneath her.

"But I loved every minute!" thought Zerelda, tying her hair back firmly. It had come loose with the dancing. "I must have been a frightful idiot before. No wonder the girls laughed at me."

She saw her old self suddenly – posing, trying to be so grown-up, piling up her hair in Lossie Laxton's terrible style, looking down on all these jolly school-girls. She wouldn't bear to think of it.

"It's *fun* to be a proper schoolgirl," she thought. "Lovely to be just myself, instead of trying to be like Lossie. What an idiot I was – far worse than Mavis, who did at least have a *real* gift!"

Mavis was getting on well. She looked forward

immensely to Zerelda's visits. Many of the third-formers had been to see her now, but she looked forward to Zerelda's visits more than to anyone else's. She thought Zerelda was wonderful – wonderful to have learnt a lesson that she, Mavis, meant to try to learn too.

It was a little comfort to Zerelda to feel that someone did think she was wonderful, even though she knew now that she wasn't. Now that Mavis had stopped talking about her voice and her marvellous future, she seemed a different kind of person – simpler, more natural, with a greater interest in other people.

"I'm never going to mention my voice again," Mavis told Zerelda. "I'm never going to say, 'when I'm an opera-singer' again. Perhaps if I'm sensible and don't boast and don't think about my voice, it'll come back."

"Oh, it'll come back, I expect," said Zerelda, comfortingly. "You did your best to get rid of it though! Oh, Mavis – you're just like me – reduced to being a schoolgirl and nothing else. But, gee, you wouldn't believe how nice it is to belong to the others, to be just as they are, and not try to make out you're too wunnerful for words!"

"Tell me about Mam'zelle and the sneezing again," begged Mavis. "You do make me laugh so. You're terribly funny when you tell things like that, Zerelda."

Zerelda was. She could not act any part, but she could tell a story in a very humorous way, and keep everyone in fits of laughter. Privately Alicia thought that that was Zerelda's real gift, the ability to be really funny – but she wasn't going to say so! She wasn't going to give Zerelda any chance of thinking herself "wunnerful" again!

The girls admired the way Zerelda gave her time so generously to Mavis. They thought a good deal more of her for taking Miss Hibbert's rather harsh ticking-off so well, and for taking to heart all she had said.

"I didn't think she had it in her," said Darrell to Sally. "I really didn't. I thought she was just an inflated balloon – and when Miss Hibbert pricked her, I thought she'd just deflate and there'd be nothing. But there *is* something after all. I like her now, don't you?"

"Well – I always did think she was very generous, and I liked her good nature," said Sally. "But then I didn't have such a dose of her silliness as you did – I didn't come back to school till so late."

"I'm glad Betty's back, aren't you?" said Darrell. "Thank goodness! Now Alicia has got someone to go round with, and she doesn't always want you and me to make a threesome. I wish Bill had a friend. She's rather on her own."

"Well – I don't mind making up a threesome with Bill sometimes," said Sally. "Though Bill doesn't *really* need a friend, you know, Darrell – honestly I think Thunder takes the place of a friend with her."

"Yes. He does," said Darrell, remembering that dark rainy night when she and Bill had walked Thunder round and round the yard. "But it would be nice for Bill if we let her go with us sometimes. She's a sport."

So Bill, to her delight, was often taken in tow by Darrell and Sally. She thought the world of Darrell. "One day I'll repay her for that night," thought Bill, a hundred times a week. "I'll never forget."

She was very happy now. Thunder was quite well.

Darrell and Sally welcomed her. She was doing well in class. And Miss Peters was simply grand!

Bill was a simple person, straightforward, natural and very loyal. These things made a great appeal to Miss Peters, who was much the same. So there grew up a real understanding betwen the form mistress and Bill, delightful to them both.

"I'm so happy here," said Bill to Darrell. "I didn't want to come – but oh, I'm so *glad* I came!"

A Lovely End to the Term!

The term was coming to an end. Darrell as usual was torn in two over her feelings about this. "I do so love going home – but I do so love being at Malory Towers!" she said to Sally.

"Well, you're lucky to have both worlds," said Sally. "So am I. I love being at home – but I love school, too. It's been a good term, hasn't it, Darrell?"

"Yes," said Darrell. "I've only had one bitter disappointment – and that was, that after all the practising I've done, and all the extra coaching I got, and the help that Molly gave me, I never played in the third match-team after all."

"Did they play the match that was cancelled?" asked Sally.

"No. The other school hadn't a free date," said Darrell. "We break up next week – so there's no chance now. That's the only thing that has really spoilt the term a bit for me – and you being so late back, of course."

"Isn't it a gorgeous afternoon?" said Sally, as they strolled out into the courtyard, and looked at the daffodils growing everywhere there, dancing in the March breeze. "There's half an hour before dinner. What shall we do?"

"Let's go out to the lacrosse field," said Darrell. "It will be lovely there. I feel restless after sitting still so long. A bit of running and catching will do us good."

Sally didn't really want to. She was not as good at games that term as usual, because she had come back so late. But she saw Darrell's eager face and put aside her own wishes.

"All right. I'll get the sticks. You go and ask for a ball," she said. They met again on the field, and were soon running and catching and passing.

They were the only ones there. Molly Ronaldson, passing by, smiled to see Darrell out there again. What a sticker she was! She really did stick to whatever she made up her mind to do. Molly liked that kind of thing.

She called to Darrell. "My goodness, you deserve to play well, Darrell! Have you heard that we are playing Barchester after all, next week – you know the match that was cancelled the half-holiday Thursday? We thought we wouldn't be able to fix it up again – but Barchester have just let us know that they can play us next Thursday – the day before we break up."

"Oh, really?" said Darrell. "Molly – any chance of my being in the reserve three again? Do say yes!"

"Well, last time, apparently, you would have actually *played* in the match, as all the reserves were to play," said Molly, "but I heard that you played the

163

fool, you and the third form, and got the half-holiday forfeited. So you wouldn't have been able to play after all."

"Yes, that's true," said Darrell. "But I haven't played the fool since. Put me in the reserve next Thursday, Molly, please do. Not that I've much hope of playing in the match this time, because everyone who was ill is all right again!"

"True," said Molly. "Well, I shall be making a new list of match-team players, and you may be in the reserve or you may not. I'm making no promises! I'll come and watch the third and fourth forms playing lacrosse on Monday afternoon. I shall only want a few players from them for the Barchester match, so it's up to you to do your best!"

"Isn't Molly marvellous!" said Darrell to Sally, her face in a glow as Molly walked off.

"Well – I think she's very good as a games captain," said Sally, who didn't get quite such wild enthusiasms as Darrell got. "Anyway – you play well on Monday, when Molly's watching, and see if you can get in the reserve again, Darrell."

So Darrell did. She was nimble and swift, she was deft at catching, unselfish in her passing, and very sure in her attack on goal. Molly was on the field, watching the various games being played there. She walked from one to another, sturdy, deliberate, her sharp eyes noting every good pass and swift rush.

That night the names of the girls in the third match-team were to be put up. The names of the reserve girls would be put below the team list. Darrell hardly dared to go up to the notice board and look to see if her name was in the reserve.

Surely it would be! Surely she had been better than

most of the fourth-formers, and certainly far better than any other third-former! She glanced hopefully but fearfully at the names of the three reserves.

Hers wasn't there! In real dismay Darrell read down the three reserve names again. No – her name was not there – not even as third reserve, which she had been before! Molly hadn't thought her good enough to put her in the reserve this time. What a terrible disappointment.

Sally came running up. "Darrell! Is your name down? Are you in the reserve?"

Darrell shook her head. "No," she said. "Not this time. Oh, Sally – I'm awfully disappointed."

Sally was too. She slipped her arm through Darrell's. "Bad luck, old thing. I *am* sorry."

"Oh well – I'm as bad as Zerelda used to be – imagining I'm good enough at lacrosse to be in the reserve for the Barchester match," said Darrell, her voice a little shaky. "Serves me right!"

"It doesn't, it doesn't!" said Sally. "You *ought* to be at least *first* reserve – yes, you ought, Darrell. You are *awfully* good – super – at lacrosse. And you've practised so hard, too."

"Don't rub it in," said Darrell, Sally's eager championship making her feel much worse. They went to the common room together. Mavis was there with Zerelda, for the first time.

"Hallo, Mavis!" cried Sally, in surprise. "I thought you weren't coming to join us again till tomorrow. I'm so glad you're back."

"Welcome home again!" said Darrell, trying to forget her disappointment. "I'm glad you're all right, Mavis. How do you feel?"

"Grand," said Mavis, in her changed voice. She no

165

longer had the deep, delightful voice she used to have. It was hoarse and had lost its lovely tone. The girls were used to it by now, but poor Mavis wasn't. She couldn't bear this horrid, creaky voice! But she had made up her mind not to grumble or complain. "I'm glad to be back, too. Sister was awfully nice to me, and it's cosy over in the san. – but I did miss all the fun and noise of school."

She coughed. "Don't talk too much all at once," said Zerelda. "You know Sister put me in charge of you – and I've got to deliver you well and healthy up to Matron tonight, before you are allowed to sleep in our dormy again!"

"I'll be all right," said Mavis. "Darrell – are you in the reserve? Zerelda said you were sure to be. I'm looking forward to seeing a match again."

"No. I'm not," said Darrell, and turned away. Zerelda looked up, surprised and sorry.

"Gee, that's too bad," she said, and then stopped as Sally frowned at her to stop her saying too much about it. Darrell was feeling it very much. She couldn't understand why Molly had left her out of the reserve this time. It didn't seem fair, after all she had said!

Darrel went out of the room. Sally didn't follow her, knowing that she wanted to be alone and get over her disappointment before she faced the rest of the form.

There came a clatter of feet down the corridor. The door burst open and the rest of the third form poured in. "I say! Where's Darrell! My goodness, has she seen the notice board?"

"Yes. She's frightfully disappointed," said Sally. The beaming third-formers looked immensely surprised.

"Disappointed!" echoed Alicia. "Why? She ought

166

to be so bucked that she's doing a war-dance round the room!"

Now it was Sally's turn to be surprised. "But why, you idiot? She's not even been put into the reserve this time!"

"No – she hasn't – because, idiot, she's in the team itself!" cried Alicia.

"Yes. Actually in the *team*!" said Bill, joyfully. "Isn't it an honour?"

Sally gasped. "Gracious! Darrell must just have looked at the names of the reserves – and not looked at the names in the *team* at all! How like her!"

"Where *is* she?" demanded Alicia, impatiently.

"Here she is!" yelled Belinda from the door. "Darrell! Come here!"

Darrell came in, looking rather subdued. She gazed round in surprise at the excited third-formers. "What's up?" she said.

"*You* are!" cried Irene, slapping her on the back. "Up on the notice board, silly! In the TEAM!"

Darrell didn't take it in. The others all crowded round her impatiently, talking at the tops of their voices.

"You're in the TEAM! Don't you understand?"

"Not in the reserve. You're PLAYING on Thursday against Barchester."

"Look at her – quite dumb. *Darrell*! Do you mean to say you only looked at the names in the reserve and not at the names in the match-team itself? Well, of all the donkeys!"

Light suddenly dawned upon Darrell. She seized Alicia's wrists joyfully. "Alicia! Do you mean it? I'm in the TEAM! Golly – I never thought of looking there."

Then there was so much shouting and congratulating and rejoicing that Matron came in to see whatever the noise was about, and to find out how Mavis was standing it.

Mavis was standing it very well. She was smacking Darrell on the back and calling out "Jolly good! Jolly good!" in a cracked but most determined voice. Her face shone with pleasure, just like the faces of the rest.

Matron went out again without being noticed. She smiled to herself. "All because someone's put into the team!" she thought. "Well, well – what a thing it is to be a schoolgirl!"

It was a lovely thing to Darrell at that moment. She thought she had never been so happy in her life before – just when she had felt so disappointed and miserable, too! She was almost in tears when she saw the pleasure and pride of the others. "Why, they must like me an awful lot!" she thought, happily. "Oh, I *do* hope I play well on Thursday. If only we can beat Barchester! We haven't for a whole year."

She could hardly wait till Thursday came – but it dawned at last, sunny and clear – the ideal day for a match. It was a home match, and as it was the day before breaking up, all girls who wished to could watch it. Most of them turned up to cheer the Barchester girls when they arrived in their coach. Then they all streamed to the field to find seats on the wooden platforms.

Darrell was nervous. She was cross with herself for this, but she couldn't help it. Molly came by, and grinned at her. "Got stage fright? Wait till you're on the field – you'll soon forget it!"

Molly was right. Once on the field, with her lacrosse stick in her hands, dancing about joyfully, all Darrell's

168

nervousness went, and she was eager for the match to begin. She was on the wing. She glanced at her opponent. She was a big, sturdy girl. Oh dear – probably she could run even faster than Darrell!

She certainly could run very fast and she was powerful too, getting the ball from Darrell nearly every time by tackling strongly and swiftly.

"Play up, Darrell! Play up!" yelled the watching third-formers, every time Darrell got the ball and sped off with it. "Oh, well passed! Oh, well caught! Play UP, Malory Towers!"

Goal to Barchester. Goal to Malory Towers. Half-time. One all. Slices of sour lemon being brought out on plates. And here was Molly beside Darrell, talking to her earnestly.

"Darrell! You're tiring the other girl out nicely. She's good, but she gets winded more quickly than you do. Watch your chance, tackle her next time she comes up, get the ball, pass to Catherine, run level, let her pass back to you and then SHOOT! Do you hear?"

"Yes. Yes, Molly," said Darrell, almost swallowing her slice of lemon in her eagerness to take it all in. "Yes – I think my opponent's tiring. I can out-run her. I'll do what you say if I can. Tell Catherine."

"I have," said Molly. "Now – there's the whistle. You're all doing well. But I think it will have to be you who does a bit of shooting this half, Darrell. The others allow themselves to be tackled too easily. Good luck."

Molly went off the field. A chorus went up from the watchers. "PLAY – UP – Malory TOWERS! PLAY UP – Malory TOWERS!"

And Malory Towers played up. Darrell and Cather-

169

ine passed beautifully to one another, and Catherine shot. Two goals to Malory Towers! Then the Barchester team got going again. Second goal to them. Two all. Fifteen minutes to play. "PLAY – UP – Malory TOWERS!"

Darrell felt the time slipping by. Two goals all – Malory Towers must shoot again before time was up. She took a fine pass, and ran with the ball in her lacrosse net. Her opponent tackled her. Darrell dodged her very neatly and sped down the field.

"Go it, DARRELL! SHOOT! SHOOT!" yelled everyone, but Darrell was too far from goal to do that. Instead, she sent the ball to Catherine, who, alas! muffed the catch, fell over, and let the enemy snatch it up from where it rolled on the ground. Then down the field rushed the Barchester wing, back towards the Malory Towers goal.

But there the goalkeeper stopped it valiantly. Hurrah! Saved again! Up the field came the ball again, and Darrell made a remarkable catch, leaping high in the air.

"Go it, DARRELL!" yelled the onlookers. Darrell ran towards the Barchester goal. Catherine kept level with her, watching carefully for a pass. When she was tackled Darrell passed the ball deftly to Catherine, making a lovely throw. Catherine caught it, but was tackled immediately. Out of the corner of her eye she saw Darrell, watching.

She threw. It was a clumsy throw, but Darrell ran to catch the ball. Once in her net she kept the ball there, dodging cleverly when she was tackled. A great cry came up from the onlookers.

"SHOOT! SHOOT! SHOOT!"

And Darrell shot. She threw the ball with all her

might at the goal. The Barchester goalkeeper came out to stop it. The ball struck her pad, then struck the goalpost – and rolled to the back of the net.

"GOAL!" What a cry went up. "Jolly good, Darrell! Fine shot! Hurrah! Three goals to two!"

Almost immediately the whistle blew for time. The two teams lined up and cheered one another. Darrell was trembling with excitement and joy. She had played in a match – she had shot the winning goal!

"Well played, young Darrell!" said Molly's voice. "You did well. That was a very fine goal."

Darrell went off to the big tea provided for the two match-teams, her heart singing. This was a great moment for her. The third-formers all crowded round her, clapping her on the shoulder, praising her, delighted that one of their own form should have shot the winning goal.

Darrell was very tired and very happy that evening. What would her father and mother and her sister Felicity say when she told them all this? Thank goodness she was seeing them tomorrow, and they would know. She could hardly wait to tell them!

All the third-formers shared in Darrell's delight. They cheered her when she came into the common-room, and she stood there blushing and embarrassed.

"Good old Darrell! So modest she didn't even think of looking in the team list for her own name – and so marvellous that she shoots the winning goal!" cried Irene, and thumped Darrell on the back so hard that she coughed.

The last day came. All the packing was done, except for a few things that the car-girls were bundling into their cars at the last minute. Goodbyes were said. Addresses were exchanged and immediately lost. Matron tried to find Belinda who had completely disappeared. Miss Potts tried to find Irene, who also seemed to have disappeared. There was a tremendous noise and confusion, in the middle of which seven boys appeared on seven horses in the drive among the cars!

"Bill! Good heavens! Here are all your brothers again!" yelled Darrell. But Bill was getting Thunder from the stables, and was not there. She appeared a moment later on her horse, and yelled with delight to see all her brothers on their horses in the drive.

"You've come to fetch me! Look at Thunder! Isn't he in good condition? Get up, Thunder! Oh, he's so pleased to see you all."

The train-girls went, and there was a little more peace. Irene wandered round lamenting that someone had taken her suitcase. Gwen went round scowling because nobody had yet come to fetch her, and she didn't want to be the last. Belinda stalked her with an open sketchbook and pencil.

"Gwen! It's my last chance! Let me sketch that scowl!"

Darrell laughed. How like Belinda to do that when her mother and father were waiting patiently in the car for her outside!

Zerelda popped up to say goodbye. How different she looked now from when she came. She wore her school hat for one thing – a thing she had said she would never do! "Goodbye," she said. "See you again next term. It's been wunnerful here. I'm glad I came – and gee! I'm glad I'm coming back!"

"Goodbye!" croaked Mavis, waving to everyone as she climbed into her car. "See you next term."

Bill galloped off with her brothers, calling a mad

172

goodbye. Mam'zelle Dupont watched her go in amazement. "In France such a thing could not happen!" she declared. "That Bill! I think at home she must let her horse sleep with her in a corner of her bedroom!"

Darrell giggled. Belinda came by with a wooden box of bath salts she had suddenly remembered leaving in the bathroom. She collided with Mam'zelle and the box fell to the floor.

A green powder covered the hall, and a green cloud rose up into the air, with a very strong smell.

"Now, Belinda, I . . ." began Mam'zelle, and then paused with her mouth wide open. She felt frantically about her plump person for her handkerchief. Just as Miss Potts came up with Miss Peters, Mam'zelle sneezed. It was one of her best efforts.

"A – WHOOOOOSH-OOOOOOO!"

"Good gracious!" said Miss Potts, startled. "I never knew anyone sn . . ."

"A-Whooooooo – " began Mam'zelle again and Miss Potts ran for shelter.

Darrell and Sally giggled helplessly. They remembered the afternoon of the trick. Darrell suddenly picked up somebody's umbrella and opened it.

"Now sneeze, Mam'zelle!" she cried, holding the umbrella over Miss Potts and Miss Peters. "I'll protect everyone!"

Darrell's mother, coming up the steps in search of her, was amazed to see this sight. Darrell flung away the umbrella joyfully and sprang at her mother. "Oh, here you are. I thought you were never coming! Sally, are you ready? Goodbye, Mam'zelle, goodbye, Potty, goodbye, Miss P, goodbye Matron. See you all next term! This has been a SUPER term!"

"Goodbye!" said Matron. "Be good."

"Goodbye," said Miss Potts and Miss Peters together. "Remember your holiday reading!"

"A-Whooosh-ooooo!" said Mam'zelle, and ran forward to wave. Gwen just saved her from falling over the open umbrella.

The car drove off. Darrell waved frantically till they were out of the front gates. Then she leaned back contentedly and began.

"Mother! Daddy! What DO you think? I played in the third match-team yesterday against Barchester School – and I shot the winning goal, Mother, I . . ."

Sally listened contentedly. Good old Darrell! She had had a lovely term and enjoyed it. She was sorry it was over. But there would be the summer term – and the autumn term – and the winter term – oh, terms and terms and terms!

"Here's the last glimpse of Malory Towers, Darrell," said Sally, suddenly. Darrell opened the window and leaned out.

"I'll soon be back, Malory Towers!" she called. "Goodbye for a little while. I'll soon be back!"

Enid Blyton
School Stories
in Armada

Malory Towers Series

First Term at Malory Towers	£2.99
Second Form at Malory Towers	£2.99
Third Year at Malory Towers	£2.99
Upper Fourth a Malory Towers	£2.99
In the Fifth at Malory Towers	£2.99
Last Term at Malory Towers	£2.99

St. Clare's Series

The Twins at St. Clare's	£2.99
The O'Sullivan Twins	£2.99
Summer Term at St. Clare's	£2.99
Second Form at St. Clare's	£2.99
Claudine at St. Clare's	£2.99
Fifth Formers at St. Clare's	£2.99

All these books are available at your local bookshop or newsagent, or can be ordered from the publisher. To order direct from the publishers just tick the titles you want and fill in the form below:

Name ————————————————————————————————

Address ——————————————————————————————

——

Send to: Collins Childrens Cash Sales
          PO Box 11
          Falmouth
          Cornwall
          TR10 9EN

Please enclose a cheque or postal order or debit my Visa/Access –

   Credit card no:

   Expiry date:

   Signature:

– to the value of the cover price plus:

UK: £1.00 for the first book, 25p for each additional book ordered.

Overseas and Eire: £2.95 service charge.

Armada reserve the right to show new retail prices on covers which may differ from those previously advertised in the text or elsewhere.

ARMADA